The Woman in the Alcove

by

Anna Katharine Green

The Echo Library 2009

Published by

The Echo Library

Echo Library
131 High St.
Teddington
Middlesex TW11 8HH

www.echo-library.com

Please report serious faults in the text to complaints@echo-library.com

ISBN 978-1-40689-403-5

THE WOMAN IN THE ALCOVE

By

ANNA KATHARINE GREEN

4

CONTENTS

I. THE WOMAN WITH THE DIAMOND 5
II. THE GLOVES 12
III. ANSON DURAND 19
IV. EXPLANATIONS 28
V. SUPERSTITION 33
VI. SUSPENSE 39
VII. NIGHT AND A VOICE 43
VIII. ARREST 53
IX. THE MOUSE NIBBLES AT THE NET 55
X. I ASTONISH THE INSPECTOR 59
XI. THE INSPECTOR ASTONISHES ME 63
XII. ALMOST 67
XIII. THE MISSING RECOMMENDATION 72
XIV. TRAPPED 78
XV. SEARS OR WELLGOOD 85
XVI. DOUBT 91
XVII. SWEETWATER IN A NEW ROLE 95
XVIII. THE CLOSED DOOR 100
XIX. THE FACE 104
XX. MOONLIGHT—AND A CLUE 106
XXI. GRIZEL! GRIZEL! 110
XXII. GUILT 115
XXIII. THE GREAT MOGUL 118

I. THE WOMAN WITH THE DIAMOND

I was, perhaps, the plainest girl in the room that night. I was also the happiest—up to one o'clock. Then my whole world crumbled, or, at least, suffered an eclipse. Why and how, I am about to relate. I was not made for love. This I had often said to myself; very often of late. In figure I am too diminutive, in face far too unbeautiful, for me to cherish expectations of this nature. Indeed, love had never entered into my plan of life, as was evinced by the nurse's diploma I had just gained after three years of hard study and severe training. I was not made for love. But if I had been; had I been gifted with height, regularity of feature, or even with that eloquence of expression which redeems all defects save those which savor of deformity, I knew well whose eye I should have chosen to please, whose heart I should have felt proud to win.

This knowledge came with a rush to my heart—(did I say heart? I should have said understanding, which is something very different)—when, at the end of the first dance, I looked up from the midst of the bevy of girls by whom I was surrounded and saw Anson Durand's fine figure emerging from that quarter of the hall where our host and hostess stood to receive their guests. His eye was roaming hither and thither and his manner was both eager and expectant. Whom was he seeking? Some one of the many bright and vivacious girls about me, for he turned almost instantly our way. But which one?

I thought I knew. I remembered at whose house I had met him first, at whose house I had seen him many times since. She was a lovely girl, witty and vivacious, and she stood at this very moment at my elbow. In her beauty lay the lure, the natural lure for a man of his gifts and striking personality. If I continued to watch, I should soon see his countenance light up under the recognition she could not fail to give him. And I was right; in another instant it did, and with a brightness there was no mistaking. But one feeling common to the human heart lends such warmth, such expressiveness to the features. How handsome it made him look, how distinguished, how everything I was not except— But what does this mean? He has passed Miss Sperry—passed her with a smile and a friendly word—and is speaking to me, singling me out, offering me his arm! He is smiling, too, not as he smiled on Miss Sperry, but more warmly, with more that is personal in it. I took his arm in a daze. The lights were dimmer than I thought; nothing was really bright except his smile. It seemed to change the world for me. I forgot that I was plain, forgot that I was small, with nothing to recommend me to the eye or heart, and let myself be drawn away, asking nothing, anticipating nothing, till I found myself alone with him in the fragrant recesses of the conservatory, with only the throb of music in our ears to link us to the scene we had left.

Why had he brought me here, into this fairyland of opalescent lights and intoxicating perfumes? What could he have to say—to show? Ah in another moment I knew. He had seized my hands, and love, ardent love, came pouring from his lips. Could it be real? Was I the object of all this feeling, I? If so, then life had changed for me indeed.

Silent from rush of emotion, I searched his face to see if this Paradise, whose gates I was thus passionately bidden to enter, was indeed a verity or only a dream born of the excitement of the dance and the charm of a scene exceptional in its splendor and picturesqueness even for so luxurious a city as New York.

But it was no mere dream. Truth and earnestness were in his manner, and his words were neither feverish nor forced. "I love you I! I need you!" So I heard, and so he soon made me believe. "You have charmed me from the first. Your tantalizing, trusting, loyal self, like no other, sweeter than any other, has drawn the heart from my breast. I have seen many women, admired many women, but you only have I loved. Will you be my wife?"

I was dazzled; moved beyond anything I could have conceived. I forgot all that I had hitherto said to myself—all that I had endeavoured to impress upon my heart when I beheld him approaching, intent, as I believed, in his search for another woman; and, confiding in his honesty, trusting entirely to his faith, I allowed the plans and purposes of years to vanish in the glamour of this new joy, and spoke the word which linked us together in a bond which half an hour before I had never dreamed would unite me to any man.

His impassioned "Mine! mine!" filled my cup to overflowing. Something of the ecstasy of living entered my soul; which, in spite of all I have suffered since, recreated the world for me and made all that went before but the prelude to the new life, the new joy.

Oh, I was happy, happy, perhaps too happy! As the conservatory filled and we passed back into the adjoining room, the glimpse I caught of myself in one of the mirrors startled me into thinking so. For had it not been for the odd color of my dress and the unique way in which I wore my hair that night, I should not have recognized the beaming girl who faced me so naively from the depths of the responsive glass. Can one be too happy? I do not know. I know that one can be too perplexed, too burdened and too sad.

Thus far I have spoken only of myself in connection with the evening's elaborate function. But though entitled by my old Dutch blood to a certain social consideration which I am happy to say never failed me, I, even in this hour of supreme satisfaction, attracted very little attention and awoke small comment. There was another woman present better calculated to do this. A fair woman, large and of a bountiful presence, accustomed to conquest, and gifted with the power of carrying off her victories with a certain lazy grace irresistibly fascinating to the ordinary man; a gorgeously appareled woman, with a diamond on her breast too vivid for most women, almost too vivid for her. I noticed this diamond early in the evening, and then I noticed her. She was not as fine as the diamond, but she was very fine, and, had I been in a less ecstatic frame of mind, I might have envied the homage she received from all the men, not excepting him upon whose arm I leaned. Later, there was no one in the world I envied less.

The ball was a private and very elegant one. There were some notable guests. One gentleman in particular was pointed out to me as an Englishman of great distinction and political importance. I thought him a very interesting man for his years, but odd and a trifle self-centered. Though greatly courted, he seemed strangely restless under the fire of eyes to which he was constantly subjected, and only happy when free to use his own in contemplation of the scene about him. Had I been less absorbed in my own happiness I might have noted sooner than I did that this contemplation was confined to such groups as gathered about the lady with the diamond. But this I failed to observe at the time, and consequently was much surprised to come upon him, at the end of one of the dances, talking With this lady in an animated and courtly manner totally opposed to the apathy, amounting to boredom, with which he had hitherto met all advances.

Yet it was not admiration for her person which he openly displayed. During the whole time he stood there his eyes seldom rose to her face; they lingered mainly-and this was what aroused my curiosity—on the great fan of ostrich plumes which this opulent beauty held against her breast. Was he desirous of seeing the great diamond she thus unconsciously (or was it consciously) shielded from his gaze? It was possible, for, as I continued to note him, he suddenly bent toward her and as quickly raised himself again with a look which was quite inexplicable to me. The lady had shifted her fan a moment and his eyes had fallen on the gem.

The next thing I recall with any definiteness was a tête-à-tête conversation which I held with my lover on a certain yellow divan at the end of one of the halls.

To the right of this divan rose a curtained recess, highly suggestive of romance, called "the alcove." As this alcove figures prominently in my story, I will pause here to describe it.

It was originally intended to contain a large group of statuary which our host, Mr. Ramsdell, had ordered from Italy to adorn his new house. He is a man of original ideas in regard to such matters, and in this instance had gone so far as to have this end of the house constructed with a special view to an advantageous display of this promised work of art. Fearing the ponderous effect of a pedestal large enough to hold such a considerable group, he had planned to raise it to the level of the eye by having the alcove floor built a few feet higher than the main one. A flight of low, wide steps connected the two, which, following the curve of the wall, added much to the beauty of this portion of the hall. The group was a failure and was never shipped; but the alcove remained, and, possessing as it did all the advantages of a room in the way of heat and light, had been turned into a miniature retreat of exceptional beauty.

The seclusion it offered extended, or so we were happy to think, to the solitary divan at its base on which Mr. Durand and I were seated. With possibly an undue confidence in the advantage of our position, we were discussing a subject interesting only to ourselves, when Mr. Durand interrupted himself to declare: "You are the woman I want, you and you only. And I want you soon. When do you think you can marry me? Within a week—if—"

Did my look stop him? I was startled. I had heard no incoherent phrase from him before.

"A week!" I remonstrated. "We take more time than that to fit ourselves for a journey or some transient pleasure. I hardly realize my engagement yet."

"You have not been thinking of it for these last two months as I have."

"No," I replied demurely, forgetting everything else in my delight at this admission.

"Nor are you a nomad among clubs and restaurants."

"No, I have a home."

"Nor do you love me as deeply as I do you."

This I thought open to argument.

"The home you speak of is a luxurious one," he continued. "I can not offer you its equal Do you expect me to?"

I was indignant.

"You know that I do not. Shall I, who deliberately chose a nurse's life when an indulgent uncle's heart and home were open to me, shrink from braving poverty with the man I love? We will begin as simply as you please—"

"No," he peremptorily put in, yet with a certain hesitancy which seemed to speak of doubts he hardly acknowledged to himself, "I will not marry you if I must expose you to privation or to the genteel poverty I hate. I love you more than you realize, and wish to make your life a happy one. I can not give you all you have been accustomed to in your rich uncle's house, but if matters prosper with me, if the chance I have built on succeeds—and it will fail or succeed tonight—you will have those comforts which love will heighten into luxuries and—and—"

He was becoming incoherent again, and this time with his eyes fixed elsewhere than on my face. Following his gaze, I discovered what had distracted his attention. The lady with the diamond was approaching us on her way to the alcove. She was accompanied by two gentlemen, both strangers to me, and her head, sparkling with brilliants, was turning from one to the other with an indolent grace. I was not surprised that the man at my side quivered and made a start as if to rise. She was a gorgeous image. In comparison with her imposing figure in its trailing robe of rich pink velvet, my diminutive frame in its sea-green gown must have looked as faded and colorless as a half-obliterated pastel.

"A striking woman," I remarked as I saw he was not likely to resume the conversation which her presence had interrupted. "And what diamond!"

The glance he cast me was peculiar.

"Did you notice it particularly?" he asked.

Astonished, for there was something very uneasy in his manner so that I half expected to see him rise and join the group he was so eagerly watching without waiting for my lips to frame a response, I quickly replied:

"It would be difficult not to notice what one would naturally expect to see only on the breast of a queen. But perhaps she is a queen. I should judge so from the homage which follows her."

His eyes sought mine. There was inquiry in them, but it was an inquiry I did not understand.

"What can you know about diamonds?" he presently demanded. "Nothing but their glitter, and glitter is not all,—the gem she wears may be a very tawdry one."

I flushed with humiliation. He was a dealer in gems—that was his business—and the check which he had put upon my enthusiasm certainly made me conscious of my own presumption. Yet I was not disposed to take back my words. I had had a better opportunity than himself for seeing this remarkable jewel, and, with the perversity of a somewhat ruffled mood, I burst forth, as soon as the color had subsided from my cheeks:

"No, no! It is glorious, magnificent. I never saw its like. I doubt if you ever have, for all your daily acquaintance with jewels. Its value must be enormous. Who is she? You seem to know her."

It was a direct question, but I received no reply. Mr. Durand's eyes had followed the lady, who had lingered somewhat ostentatiously on the top step and they did not return to me till she had vanished with her companions behind the long plush curtain which partly veiled the entrance. By this time he had forgotten my words, if he had ever heard them and it was with the forced animation of one whose thoughts are elsewhere that he finally returned to the old plea:

When would I marry him? If he could offer me a home in a month—and he would know by to-morrow if he could do so—would I come to him then? He would not say in a week; that was perhaps to soon; but in a month? Would I not promise to be his in a month?

What I answered I scarcely recall. His eyes had stolen back to the alcove and mine had followed them. The gentlemen who had accompanied the lady inside were coming out again, but others were advancing to take their places, and soon she was engaged in holding a regular court in this favored retreat.

Why should this interest me? Why should I notice her or look that way at all? Because Mr. Durand did? Possibly. I remember that for all his ardent love-making, I felt a little piqued that he should divide his attentions in this way. Perhaps I thought that for this evening, at least, he might have been blind to a mere coquette's fascinations.

I was thus doubly engaged in listening to my lover's words and in watching the various gentlemen who went up and down the steps, when a former partner advanced and reminded me that I had promised him a waltz. Loath to leave Mr. Durand, yet seeing no way of excusing myself to Mr. Fox, I cast an appealing glance at the former and was greatly chagrined to find him already on his feet.

"Enjoy your dance," he cried; "I have a word to say to Mrs. Fairbrother," and was gone before my new partner had taken me on his arm.

Was Mrs. Fairbrother the lady with the diamond? Yes; as I turned to enter the parlor with my partner, I caught a glimpse of Mr. Durand's tall figure just disappearing from the step behind the sage-green curtains.

"Who is Mrs. Fairbrother?" I inquired of Mr. Fox at the end of the dance.

Mr. Fox, who is one of society's perennial beaux, knows everybody.

"She is—well, she was Abner Fairbrother's wife. You know Fairbrother, the millionaire who built that curious structure on Eighty-sixth Street. At present they are living apart—an amicable understanding, I believe. Her diamond makes her conspicuous. It is one of the most remarkable stones in New York, perhaps in the United States. Have you observed it?"

"Yes—that is, at a distance. Do you think her very handsome?"

"Mrs. Fairbrother? She's called so, but she's not my style." Here he gave me a killing glance. "I admire women of mind and heart. They do not need to wear jewels worth an ordinary man's fortune."

I looked about for an excuse to leave this none too desirable partner.

"Let us go back into the long hall," I urged. "The ceaseless whirl of these dancers is making me dizzy."

With the ease of a gallant man he took me on his arm and soon we were promenading again in the direction of the alcove. A passing glimpse of its interior was afforded me as we turned to retrace our steps in front of the yellow divan. The lady with the diamond was still there. A fold of the superb pink velvet she wore protruded across the gap made by the half-drawn curtains, just as it had done a half-hour before. But it was impossible to see her face or who was with her. What I could see, however, and did, was the figure of a man leaning against the wall at the foot of the steps. At first I thought this person unknown to me, then I perceived that he was no other than the chief guest of the evening, the Englishman of whom I have previously spoken. His expression had altered. He looked now both anxious and absorbed, particularly anxious and particularly absorbed; so much so that I was not surprised that no one ventured to approach him. Again I wondered and again I asked myself for whom or for what he was waiting. For Mr. Durand to leave this lady's presence? No, no, I would not believe that. Mr. Durand could not be there still; yet some women make it difficult for a man to leave them and, realizing this, I could not forbear casting a parting glance behind me as, yielding to Mr. Fox's importunities, I turned toward the supper-room. It showed me the Englishman in the act of lifting two cups of coffee from a small table standing near the reception-room door. As his manner plainly betokened whither he was bound with this refreshment, I felt all my uneasiness vanish, and was able to take my seat at one of the small tables with which the supper-room was filled, and for a few minutes, at least, lend an ea to Mr. Fox's vapid compliments and trite opinions. Then my attention wandered.

I had not moved nor had I shifted my gaze from the scene before me the ordinary scene of a gay and well-filled supper-room, yet I found myself looking, as if through a mist I had not even seen develop, at something as strange, unusual and remote as any phantasm, yet distinct enough in its outlines for me to get a decided impression of a square of light surrounding the figure of a man in a peculiar pose not easily imagined and not easily described. It all passed in an instant, and I sat staring at the window opposite me with the feeling of one who has just seen a vision. Yet almost immediately I forgot the whole occurrence in my anxiety as to Mr. Durand's whereabouts. Certainly he was amusing himself very much elsewhere or he would have found an opportunity of joining me long before this. He was not even in sight, and I grew weary of the endless menu and the senseless chit chat of my companion, and, finding him amenable to my whims, rose from my seat at table and made my way to a group of acquaintances standing just outside the supper-room door. As I listened to their greetings some impulse led me to cast another glance down the hall toward the alcove. A man— a waiter—was issuing from it in a rush. Bad news was in his face, and as his eyes encountered those of Mr. Ramsdell, who was advancing hurriedly to meet him, he plunged down the steps with a cry which drew a crowd about the two in an instant. What was it? What had happened?

Mad with an anxiety I did not stop to define, I rushed toward this group now swaying from side to side in irrepressible excitement, when suddenly everything swam before me and I fell in a swoon to the floor. Some one had shouted aloud:

"Mrs. Fairbrother has been murdered and her diamond stolen! Lock the doors!"

II. THE GLOVES

I must have remained insensible for many minutes, for when I returned to full consciousness the supper-room was empty and the two hundred guests I had left seated at table were gathered in agitated groups about the hall. This was what I first noted; not till afterward did I realize my own situation. I was lying on a couch in a remote corner of this same hall and beside me, but not looking at me, stood my lover, Mr. Durand.

How he came to know my state and find me in the general disturbance I did not stop to inquire. It was enough for me at that moment to look up and see him so near. Indeed, the relief was so great, the sense of his protection so comforting that I involuntarily stretched out my hand in gratitude toward him, but, failing to attract his attention, slipped to the floor and took my stand at his side. This roused him and he gave me a look which steadied me, in spite of the thrill of surprise with which I recognized his extreme pallor and a certain peculiar hesitation in his manner not at all natural to it.

Meanwhile, some words uttered near us were slowly making their way into my benumbed brain. The waiter who had raised the first alarm was endeavoring to describe to an importunate group in advance of us what he had come upon in that murderous alcove.

"I was carrying about a tray of ices," he was saying, "and seeing the lady sitting there, went up. I had expected to find the place full of gentlemen, but she was all alone, and did not move as I picked my way over her long train. The next moment I had dropped ices, tray and all. I bad come face to face with her and seen that she was dead. She had been stabbed and robbed. There was no diamond on her breast, but there was blood."

A hubbub of disordered sentences seasoned with horrified cries followed this simple description. Then a general movement took place in the direction of the alcove, during which Mr. Durand stooped to my ear and whispered:

"We must get out of this. You are not strong enough to stand such excitement. Don't you think we can escape by the window over there?"

"What, without wraps and in such a snowstorm?" I protested. "Besides, uncle will be looking for me. He came with me, you know."

An expression of annoyance, or was it perplexity, crossed Mr. Durand's face, and he made a movement as if to leave me.

"I must go," he began, but stopped at my glance of surprise and assumed a different air—one which became him very much better. "Pardon me, dear, I will take you to your uncle. This—this dreadful tragedy, interrupting so gay a scene, has quite upset me. I was always sensitive to the sight, the smell, even to the very mention of the word blood."

So was I, but not to the point of cowardice. But then I had not just come from an interview with the murdered woman. Her glances, her smiles, the lift of her eyebrows were not fresh memories to me. Some consideration was certainly due him for the shock he must be laboring under. Yet I did not know how to keep back the vital question.

"Who did it? You must have heard some one say."

"I have heard nothing," was his somewhat fierce rejoinder. Then, as I made a move, "What you do not wish to follow the crowd there?"

"I wish to find my uncle, and he is in that crowd."

Mr. Durand said nothing further, and together we passed down the hall. A strange mood pervaded my mind. Instead of wishing to fly a scene which under ordinary conditions would have filled me with utter repugnance, I felt a desire to see and hear everything. Not from curiosity, such as moved most of the people about me, but because of some strong instinctive feeling I could not understand; as if it were my heart which had been struck, and my fate which was trembling in the balance.

We were consequently among the first to hear such further details as were allowed to circulate among the now well-nigh frenzied guests. No one knew the perpetrator of the deed nor did there appear to be any direct evidence calculated to fix his identity. Indeed, the sudden death of this beautiful woman in the midst of festivity might have been looked upon as suicide, if the jewel had not been missing from her breast and the instrument of death removed from the wound. So far, the casual search which had been instituted had failed to produce this weapon; but the police would be here soon and then something would be done. As to the means of entrance employed by the assassin, there seemed to be but one opinion. The alcove contained a window opening upon a small balcony. By this he had doubtless entered and escaped. The long plush curtains which, during the early part of the evening, had remained looped back on either side of the casement, were found at the moment of the crime's discovery closely drawn together. Certainly a suspicious circumstance. However, the question was one easily settled. If any one had approached by the balcony there would be marks in the snow to show it. Mr. Ramsdell had gone out to see. He would be coming back soon.

"Do you think this a probable explanation of the crime?" I demanded of Mr. Durand at this juncture. "If I remember rightly this window overlooks the carriage drive; it must, therefore, be within plain sight of the door through which some three hundred guests have passed to-night. How could any one climb to such a height, lift the window and step in without being seen?"

"You forget the awning." He spoke quickly and with unexpected vivacity. "The awning runs up very near this window and quite shuts it off from the sight of arriving guests. The drivers of departing carriages could see it if they chanced to glance back. But their eyes are usually on their horses in such a crowd. The probabilities are against any of them having looked up." His brow had cleared; a weight seemed removed from his mind. "When I went into the alcove to see Mrs. Fairbrother, she was sitting in a chair near this window looking out. I remember the effect of her splendor against the snow sifting down in a steady stream behind her. The pink velvet—the soft green of the curtains on either side—her brilliants—and the snow for a background! Yes, the murderer came in that way. Her figure would be plain to any one outside, and if she moved and the diamond shone—Don't you see what a probable theory it is? There must be ways by which a desperate man might reach that balcony. I believe—"

How eager he was and with what a look he turned when the word came filtering through the crowd that, though footsteps had been found in the snow pointing directly toward the balcony, there was none on the balcony itself, proving, as any one could see, that the attack had not come from without, since no one could enter the alcove by the window without stepping on the balcony.

"Mr. Durand has suspicions of his own," I explained determinedly to myself. "He met some one going in as he stepped out. Shall I ask him to name this person?" No, I did not have the courage; not while his face wore so stern a look and was so resolutely turned away.

The next excitement was a request from Mr. Ramsdell for us all to go into the drawing-room. This led to various cries from hysterical lips, such as, "We are going to be searched!" "He believes the thief and murderer to be still in the house!" "Do you see the diamond on me?" "Why don't they confine their suspicions to the favored few who were admitted to the alcove?"

"They will," remarked some one close to my ear.

But quickly as I turned I could not guess from whom the comment came. Possibly from a much beflowered, bejeweled, elderly dame, whose eyes were fixed on Mr. Durand's averted face. If so, she received a defiant look from mine, which I do not believe she forgot in a hurry.

Alas! it was not the only curious, I might say searching glance I surprised directed against him as we made our way to where I could see my uncle struggling to reach us from a short side hall. The whisper seemed to have gone about that Mr. Durand had been the last one to converse with Mrs. Fairbrother prior to the tragedy.

In time I had the satisfaction of joining my uncle. He betrayed great relief at the sight of me, and, encouraged by his kindly smile, I introduced Mr. Durand. My conscious air must have produced its impression, for he turned a startled and inquiring look upon my companion, then took me resolutely on his own arm, saying:

"There is likely to be some unpleasantness ahead for all of us. I do not think the police will allow any one to go till that diamond has been looked for. This is a very serious matter, dear. So many think the murderer was one of the guests."

"I think so, too," said I. But why I thought so or why I should say so with such vehemence, I do not know even now.

My uncle looked surprised.

"You had better not advance any opinions," he advised. "A lady like yourself should have none on a subject so gruesome. I shall never cease regretting bringing you here tonight. I shall seize on the first opportunity to take you home. At present we are supposed to await the action of our host."

"He can not keep all these people here long," I ventured.

"No; most of us will be relieved soon. Had you not better get your wraps so as to be ready to go as soon as he gives the word?"

"I should prefer to have a peep at the people in the drawing-room first," was my perverse reply. "I don't know why I want to see them, but I do; and, uncle, I might as well tell you now that I engaged myself to Mr. Durand this evening—the gentleman with me when you first came up."

"You have engaged yourself to—to this man—to marry him, do you mean?"

I nodded, with a sly look behind to see if Mr. Durand were near enough to hear. He was not, and I allowed my enthusiasm to escape in a few quick words.

"He has chosen me," I said, "the plainest, most uninteresting puss in the whole city." My uncle smiled. "And I believe he loves me; at all events, I know that I love him."

My uncle sighed, while giving me the most affectionate of glances.

"It's a pity you should have come to this understanding to-night," said he. "He's an acquaintance of the murdered woman, and it is only right for you to know that you will have to leave him behind when you start for home. All who have been seen entering that alcove this evening will necessarily be detained here till the coroner arrives."

My uncle and I strolled toward the drawing-room and as we did so we passed the library. It held but one occupant, the Englishman. He was seated before a table, and his appearance was such as precluded any attempt at intrusion, even if one had been so disposed. There was a fixity in his gaze and a frown on his powerful forehead which bespoke a mind greatly agitated. It was not for me to read that mind, much as it interested me, and I passed on, chatting, as if I had not the least desire to stop.

I can not say how much time elapsed before my uncle touched me on the arm with the remark:

"The police are here in full force. I saw a detective in plain clothes look in here a minute ago. He seemed to have his eye on you. There he is again! What can he want? No, don't turn; he's gone away now."

Frightened as I had never been in all my life, I managed to keep my head up and maintain an indifferent aspect. What, as my uncle said, could a detective want of me? I had nothing to do with the crime; not in the remotest way could I be said to be connected with it; why, then, had I caught the attention of the police? Looking about, I sought Mr. Durand. He had left me on my uncle's coming up, but had remained, as I supposed, within sight. But at this moment he was nowhere to be seen. Was I afraid on his account? Impossible; yet—

Happily just then the word was passed about that the police had given orders that, with the exception of such as had been requested to remain to answer questions, the guests generally should feel themselves at liberty to depart.

The time had now come to take a stand and I informed my uncle, to his evident chagrin, that I should not leave as long as any excuse could be found for staying.

He said nothing at the time, but as the noise of departing carriages gradually lessened and the great hall and drawing-rooms began to wear a look of desertion he at last ventured on this gentle protest:

"You have more pluck, Rita, than I supposed. Do you think it wise to stay on here? Will not people imagine that you have been requested to do so? Look at those waiters hanging about in the different doorways. Run up and put on your wraps. Mr. Durand will come to the house fast enough as soon as he is released. I give you leave to sit up for him if you will; only let us leave this place before that impertinent little man dares to come around again," he artfully added.

But I stood firm, though somewhat moved by his final suggestion; and, being a small tyrant in my way, at least with him, I carried my point.

Suddenly my anxiety became poignant. A party of men, among whom I saw Mr. Durand, appeared at the end of the hall, led by a very small but self-important personage whom my uncle immediately pointed out as the detective who had twice come to the door near which I stood. As this man looked up and saw me still there, a look of relief crossed his face, and, after a word or two with another stranger of seeming authority, he detached himself from the group he had ushered upon the scene, and, approaching me respectfully enough, said with a deprecatory glance at my uncle whose frown he doubtless understood:

"Miss Van Arsdale, I believe?"

I nodded, too choked to speak.

"I am sorry, Madam, if you were expecting to go. Inspector Dalzell has arrived and would like to speak to you. Will you step into one of these rooms? Not the library, but any other. He will come to you as quickly as he can."

I tried to carry it off bravely and as if I saw nothing in this summons which was unique or alarming. But I succeeded only in dividing a wavering glance between him and the group of men of which he had just formed a part. In the latter were several gentlemen whom I had noted in Mrs. Fairbrother's train early in the evening and a few strangers, two of whom were officials. Mr. Durand was with the former, and his expression did not encourage me.

"The affair is very serious," commented the detective on leaving me. "That's our excuse for any trouble we may be putting you to." I clutched my uncle's arm.

"Where shall we go?" I asked. "The drawing-room is too large. In this hall my eyes are for ever traveling in the direction of the alcove. Don't you know some little room? Oh, what, what can he want of me?"

"Nothing serious, nothing important," blustered my good uncle. "Some triviality such as you can answer in a moment. A little room? Yes, I know one, there, under the stairs. Come, I will find the door for you. Why did we ever come to this wretched ball?"

I had no answer for this. Why, indeed!

My uncle, who is a very patient man, guided me to the place he had picked out, without adding a word to the ejaculation in which he had just allowed his impatience to expend itself. But once seated within, and out of the range of peering eyes and listening ears, he allowed a sigh to escape him which expressed the fullness of his agitation.

"My dear," he began, and stopped. "I feel—" here he again came to a pause—"that you should know—"

"What?" I managed to ask.

"That I do not like Mr. Durand and—that others do not like him."

"Is it because of something you knew about him before to-night?"

He made no answer.

"Or because he was seen, like many other gentlemen, talking with that woman some time before—a long time before—she was attacked for her diamond and murdered?"

"Pardon me, my dear, he was the last one seen talking to her. Some one may yet be found who went in after he came out, but as yet he is considered the last. Mr. Ramsdell himself told me so."

"It makes no difference," I exclaimed, in all the heat of my long-suppressed agitation. "I am willing to stake my life on his integrity and honor. No man could talk to me as he did early this evening with any vile intentions at heart. He was interested, no doubt, like many others, in one who had the name of being a captivating woman, but—"

I paused in sudden alarm. A look had crossed my uncle's face which assured me that we were no longer alone. Who could have entered so silently? In some trepidation I turned to see. A gentleman was standing in the doorway, who smiled as I met his eye.

"Is this Miss Van Arsdale?" he asked.

Instantly my courage, which had threatened to leave me, returned and I smiled.

"I am," said I. "Are you the inspector?"

"Inspector Dalzell," he explained with a bow, which included my uncle.

Then he closed the door.

"I hope I have not frightened you," he went on, approaching me with a gentlemanly air. "A little matter has come up concerning which I mean to be perfectly frank with you. It may prove to be of trivial importance; if so, you will pardon my disturbing you. Mr. Durand—you know him?"

"I am engaged to him," I declared before poor uncle could raise his hand.

"You are engaged to him. Well, that makes it difficult, and yet, in some respects, easier for me to ask a certain question."

It must have made it more difficult than easy, for he did not proceed to put this question immediately, but went on:

"You know that Mr. Durand visited Mrs. Fairbrother in the alcove a little while before her death?"

"I have been told so."

"He was seen to go in, but I have not yet found any one who saw him come out; consequently we have been unable to fix the exact minute when he did so. What is the matter, Miss Van Arsdale? You want to say something?"

"No, no," I protested, reconsidering my first impulse. Then, as I met his look, "He can probably tell you that himself. I am sure he would not hesitate."

"We shall ask him later," was the inspector's response. "Meanwhile, are you ready to assure me that since that time he has not intrusted you with a little article to keep—No, no, I do not mean the diamond," he broke in, in very evident dismay, as I fell back from him in irrepressible indignation and alarm. "The diamond—well, we shall look for that later; it is another article we are in search of now, one which Mr. Durand might very well have taken in his hand without realizing just what he was doing. As it is important for us to find this article, and as it is one he might very naturally have passed over to you when he found himself in the hall with it in his hand, I have ventured to ask you if this surmise is correct."

"It is not," I retorted fiercely, glad that I could speak from my very heart. "He has given me nothing to keep for him. He would not—"

Why that peculiar look in the inspector's eye? Why did he reach out for a chair and seat me in it before he took up my interrupted sentence and finished it?

"—would not give you anything to hold which had belonged to another woman? Miss Van Arsdale, you do not know men. They do many things which a young, trusting girl like yourself would hardly expect from them."

"Not Mr. Durand," I maintained stoutly.

"Perhaps not; let us hope not." Then, with a quick change of manner, he bent toward me, with a sidelong look at uncle, and, pointing to my gloves, remarked: "You wear gloves. Did you feel the need of two pairs, that you carry another in that pretty bag hanging from your arm?"

I started, looked down, and then slowly drew up into my hand the bag he had mentioned. The white finger of a glove was protruding from the top. Any one could see it; many probably had. What did it mean? I had brought no extra pair with me.

"This is not mine," I began, faltering into silence as I perceived my uncle turn and walk a step or two away.

"The article we are looking for," pursued the inspector, "is a pair of long, white gloves, supposed to have been worn by Mrs. Fairbrother when she entered the alcove. Do you mind showing me those, a finger of which I see?"

I dropped the bag into his hand. The room and everything in it was whirling around me. But when I noted what trouble it was to his clumsy fingers to open it, my senses returned and, reaching for the bag, I pulled it open and snatched out the gloves. They had been hastily rolled up and some of the fingers were showing.

"Let me have them," he said.

With quaking heart and shaking fingers I handed over the gloves.

"Mrs. Fairbrother's hand was not a small one," he observed as he slowly unrolled them. "Yours is. We can soon tell—"

But that sentence was never finished. As the gloves fell open in his grasp he uttered a sudden, sharp ejaculation and I a smothered shriek. An object of superlative brilliancy had rolled out from them. The diamond! the gem which men said was worth a king's ransom, and which we all knew had just cost a life.

III. ANSON DURAND

With benumbed senses and a dismayed heart, I stared at the fallen jewel as at some hateful thing menacing both my life and honor.

"I have had nothing to do with it," I vehemently declared. "I did not put the gloves in my bag, nor did I know the diamond was in them. I fainted at the first alarm, and—"

"There! there! I know," interposed the inspector kindly. "I do not doubt you in the least; not when there is a man to doubt. Miss Van Arsdale, you had better let your uncle take you home. I will see that the hall is cleared for you. Tomorrow I may wish to talk to you again, but I will spare you all further importunity tonight."

I shook my head. It would require more courage to leave at that moment than to stay. Meeting the inspector's eye firmly, I quietly declared,

"If Mr. Durand's good name is to suffer in any way, I will not forsake him. I have confidence in his integrity, if you have not. It was not his hand, but one much more guilty, which dropped this jewel into the bag."

"So! so! do not be too sure of that, little woman. You had better take your lesson at once. It will be easier for you, and more wholesome for him."

Here he picked up the jewel.

"Well, they said it was a wonder!" he exclaimed, in sudden admiration. "I am not surprised, now that I have seen a great gem, at the famous stories I have read of men risking life and honor for their possession. If only no blood had been shed!"

"Uncle! uncle!" I wailed aloud in my agony.

It was all my lips could utter, but to uncle it was enough. Speaking for the first time, he asked to have a passage made for us, and when the inspector moved forward to comply, he threw his arm about me, and was endeavoring to find fitting words with which to fill up the delay, when a short altercation was heard from the doorway, and Mr. Durand came rushing in, followed immediately by the inspector.

His first look was not at myself, but at the bag, which still hung from my arm. As I noted this action, my whole inner self seemed to collapse, dragging my happiness down with it. But my countenance remained unchanged, too much so, it seems; for when his eye finally rose to my face, he found there what made him recoil and turn with something like fierceness on his companion.

"You have been talking to her," he vehemently protested. "Perhaps you have gone further than that. What has happened here? I think I ought to know. She is so guileless, Inspector Dalzell; so perfectly free from all connection with this crime. Why have you shut her up here, and plied her with questions, and made her look at me with such an expression, when all you have against me is just what you have against some half-dozen others,—that I was weak enough, or unfortunate enough, to spend a few minutes with that unhappy woman in the alcove before she died?"

"It might be well if Miss Van Arsdale herself would answer you," was the inspector's quiet retort. "What you have said may constitute all that we have against you, but it is not all we have against her."

I gasped, not so much at this seeming accusation, the motive of which I believed myself to understand, but at the burning blush with which it was received by Mr. Durand.

"What do you mean?" he demanded, with certain odd breaks in his voice. "What can you have against her?"

"A triviality," returned the inspector, with a look in my direction that was, I felt, not to be mistaken.

"I do not call it a triviality," I burst out. "It seems that Mrs. Fairbrother, for all her elaborate toilet, was found without gloves on her arms. As she certainly wore them on entering the alcove, the police have naturally been looking for them. And where do you think they have found them? Not in the alcove with her, not in the possession of the man who undoubtedly carried them away with him, but—"

"I know, I know," Mr. Durand hoarsely put in. "You need not say any more. Oh, my poor Rita! what have I brought upon you by my weakness?"

"Weakness!"

He started; I started; my voice was totally unrecognizable.

"I should give it another name," I added coldly.

For a moment he seemed to lose heart, then he lifted his head again, and looked as handsome as when he pleaded for my hand in the little conservatory.

"You have that right," said he; "besides, weakness at such a time, and under such an exigency, is little short of wrong. It was unmanly in me to endeavor to secrete these gloves; more than unmanly for me to choose for their hiding-place the recesses of an article belonging exclusively to yourself. I acknowledge it, Rita, and shall meet only my just punishment if you deny me in the future both your sympathy and regard. But you must let me assure you and these gentlemen also, one of whom can make it very unpleasant for me, that consideration for you, much more than any miserable anxiety about myself, lay at the bottom of what must strike you all as an act of unpardonable cowardice. From the moment I learned of this woman's murder in the alcove, where I had visited her, I realized that every one who had been seen to approach her within a half-hour of her death would be subjected to a more or less rigid investigation, and I feared, if her gloves were found in my possession, some special attention might be directed my way which would cause you unmerited distress. So, yielding to an impulse which I now recognize as a most unwise, as well as unworthy one, I took advantage of the bustle about us, and of the insensibility into which you had fallen, to tuck these miserable gloves into the bag I saw lying on the floor at your side. I do not ask your pardon. My whole future life shall be devoted to winning that; I simply wish to state a fact."

"Very good!" It was the inspector who spoke; I could not have uttered a word to save my life. "Perhaps you will now feel that you owe it to this young lady to add how you came to have these gloves in your possession?"

"Mrs. Fairbrother handed them to me."

"Handed them to you?"

"Yes, I hardly know why myself. She asked me to take care of them for her. I know that this must strike you as a very peculiar statement. It was my realization of the unfavorable effect it could not fail to produce upon those who heard it, which made me dread any interrogation on the subject. But I assure you it was as I say. She put the gloves into my hand while I was talking to her, saying they incommoded her."

"And you?"

"Well, I held them for a few minutes, then I put them in my pocket, but quite automatically, and without thinking very much about it. She was a woman accustomed to have her own way. People seldom questioned it, I judge."

Here the tension about my throat relaxed, and I opened my lips to speak. But the inspector, with a glance of some authority, forestalled me.

"Were the gloves open or rolled up when she offered them to you?"

"They were rolled up."

"Did you see her take them off?"

"Assuredly."

"And roll them up?"

"Certainly."

"After which she passed them over to you?"

"Not immediately. She let them lie in her lap for a while."

"While you talked?"

Mr. Durand bowed.

"And looked at the diamond?"

Mr. Durand bowed for the second time.

"Had you ever seen so fine a diamond before?"

"No."

"Yet you deal in precious stones?"

"That is my business."

"And are regarded as a judge of them?"

"I have that reputation."

"Mr. Durand, would you know this diamond if you saw it?"

"I certainly should."

"The setting was an uncommon one, I hear."

"Quite an unusual one."

The inspector opened his hand.

"Is this the article?"

"Good God! Where—"

"Don't you know?"

"I do not."

The inspector eyed him gravely.

"Then I have a bit of news for you. It was hidden in the gloves you took from Mrs. Fairbrother. Miss Van Arsdale was present at their unrolling."

Do we live, move, breathe at certain moments? It hardly seems so. I know that I was conscious of but one sense, that of seeing; and of but one faculty, that of judgment. Would he flinch, break down, betray guilt, or simply show astonishment? I chose to believe it was the latter feeling only which informed his slowly whitening and disturbed features. Certainly it was all his words expressed, as his glances flew from the stone to the gloves, and back again to the inspector's face.

"I can not believe it. I can not believe it." And his hand flew wildly to his forehead.

"Yet it is the truth, Mr. Durand, and one you have now to face. How will you do this? By any further explanations, or by what you may consider a discreet silence?"

"I have nothing to explain,—the facts are as I have stated."

The inspector regarded him with an earnestness which made my heart sink.

"You can fix the time of this visit, I hope; tell us, I mean, just when you left the alcove. You must have seen some one who can speak for you."

"I fear not."

Why did he look so disturbed and uncertain?

"There were but few persons in the hall just then," he went on to explain. "No one was sitting on the yellow divan."

"You know where you went, though? Whom you saw and what you did before the alarm spread?"

"Inspector, I am quite confused. I did go somewhere; I did not remain in that part of the hall. But I can tell you nothing definite, save that I walked about, mostly among strangers, till the cry rose which sent us all in one direction and me to the side of my fainting sweetheart."

"Can you pick out any stranger you talked to, or any one who might have noted you during this interval? You see, for the sake of this little woman, I wish to give you every chance."

"Inspector, I am obliged to throw myself on your mercy. I have no such witness to my innocence as you call for. Innocent people seldom have. It is only the guilty who take the trouble to provide for such contingencies."

This was all very well, if it had been uttered with a straightforward air and in a clear tone. But it was not. I who loved him felt that it was not, and consequently was more or less prepared for the change which now took place in the inspector's manner. Yet it pierced me to the heart to observe this change, and I instinctively dropped my face into my hands when I saw him move toward Mr. Durand with some final order or word of caution.

Instantly (and who can account for such phenomena?) there floated into view before my retina a reproduction of the picture I had seen, or imagined myself to have seen, in the supper-room; and as at that time it opened before me an unknown vista quite removed from the surrounding scene, so it did now, and I beheld again in faint outlines, and yet with the effect of complete distinctness, a square of light through which appeared an open passage partly shut off from view by a half-lifted curtain and the tall figure of a man holding back this curtain and gazing, or seeming to gaze, at his own breast, on which he had already laid one quivering finger.

What did it mean? In the excitement of the horrible occurrence which had engrossed us all, I had forgotten this curious experience; but on feeling anew the vague sensation of shock and expectation which seemed its natural accompaniment, I became conscious of a sudden conviction that the picture which had opened before me in the supper-room was the result of a reflection in a glass or mirror of something then going on in a place not otherwise within the reach of my vision; a reflection, the importance of which I suddenly realized when I recalled at what a critical moment it had occurred. A man in a state of dread looking at his breast, within five minutes of the stir and rush of the dreadful event which had marked this evening!

A hope, great as the despair in which I had just been sunk, gave me courage to drop my hands and advance impetuously toward the inspector.

"Don't speak, I pray; don't judge any of us further till you have heard what I have to say."

In great astonishment and with an aspect of some severity, he asked me what I had to say now which I had not had the opportunity of saying before. I replied with all the passion of a forlorn hope that it was only at this present moment I remembered a fact which might have a very decided bearing on this case; and, detecting evidences, as I thought, of relenting on his part, I backed up this statement by an entreaty for a few words with him apart, as the matter I had to tell was private and possibly too fanciful for any ear but his own.

He looked as if he apprehended some loss of valuable time, but, touched by the involuntary gesture of appeal with which I supplemented my request, he led me into a corner, where, with just an encouraging glance toward Mr. Durand, who seemed struck dumb by my action, I told the inspector of that momentary picture which I had seen reflected in what I was now sure was some window-pane or mirror.

"It was at a time coincident, or very nearly coincident, with the perpetration of the crime you are now investigating," I concluded. "Within five minutes afterward came the shout which roused us all to what had happened in the alcove. I do not know what passage I saw or what door or even what figure; but the latter, I am sure, was that of the guilty man. Something in the outline (and it was the outline only I could catch) expressed an emotion incomprehensible to me at the moment, but which, in my remembrance, impresses me as that of fear and dread. It was not the entrance to the alcove I beheld—that would have struck me at once—but some other opening which I might recognize if I saw it. Can not that opening be found, and may it not give a clue to the man I saw skulking through it with terror and remorse in his heart?"

"Was this figure, when you saw it, turned toward you or away?" the inspector inquired with unexpected interest.

"Turned partly away. He was going from me."

"And you sat—where?"

"Shall I show you?"

The inspector bowed, then with a low word of caution turned to my uncle.

"I am going to take this young lady into the hall for a moment, at her own request. May I ask you and Mr. Durand to await me here?"

Without pausing for reply, he threw open the door and presently we were pacing the deserted supper-room, seeking the place where I had sat. I found it almost by a miracle,—everything being in great disorder. Guided by my bouquet, which I had left behind me in my escape from the table, I laid hold of the chair before which it lay, and declared quite confidently to the inspector:

"This is where I sat."

Naturally his glance and mine both flew to the opposite wall. A window was before us of an unusual size and make. Unlike any which had ever before come under my observation, it swung on a pivot, and, though shut at the present moment, might very easily, when opened, present its huge pane at an angle capable of catching reflections from some of the many mirrors decorating the reception-room situated diagonally across the hall. As all the doorways on this lower floor were of unusual width, an open path was offered, as it were, for these reflections to pass, making it possible for scenes to be imaged here which, to the persons involved, would seem as safe from any one's scrutiny as if they were taking place in the adjoining house.

As we realized this, a look passed between us of more than ordinary significance. Pointing to the window, the inspector turned to a group of waiters watching us from the other side of the room and asked if it had been opened that evening.

The answer came quickly.

"Yes, sir,—just before the—the—"

"I understand," broke in the inspector; and, leaning over me, he whispered: "Tell me again exactly what you thought you saw."

But I could add little to my former description. "Perhaps you can tell me this," he kindly persisted. "Was the picture, when you saw it, on a level with your eye, or did you have to lift your head in order to see it?"

"It was high up,—in the air, as it were. That seemed its oddest feature."

The inspector's mouth took a satisfied curve. "Possibly I might identify the door and passage, if I saw them," I suggested.

"Certainly, certainly," was his cheerful rejoinder; and, summoning one of his men, he was about to give some order, when his impulse changed, and he asked if I could draw.

I assured him, in some surprise, that I was far from being an adept in that direction, but that possibly I might manage a rough sketch; whereupon he pulled a pad and pencil from his pocket and requested me to make some sort of attempt to reproduce, on paper, my memory of this passage and the door.

My heart was beating violently, and the pencil shook in my hand, but I knew that it would not do for me to show any hesitation in fixing for all eyes what, unaccountably to myself, continued to be perfectly plain to my own. So I endeavored to do as he bade me, and succeeded, to some extent, for he uttered a slight ejaculation at one of its features, and, while duly expressing his thanks, honored me with a very sharp look.

"Is this your first visit to this house?" he asked.

"No; I have been here before."

"In the evening, or in the afternoon?"

"In the afternoon."

"I am told that the main entrance is not in use to-night."

"No. A side door is provided for occasions like the present. Guests entering there find a special hall and staircase, by which they can reach the upstairs dressing-rooms, without crossing the main hall. Is that what you mean?"

"Yes, that is what I mean."

I stared at him in wonder. What lay back of such questions as these?

"You came in, as others did, by this side entrance," he now proceeded. "Did you notice, as you turned to go up stairs, an arch opening into a small passageway at your left?"

"I did not," I began, flushing, for I thought I understood him now. "I was too eager to reach the dressing-room to look about me."

"Very well," he replied; "I may want to show you that arch."

The outline of an arch, backing the figure we were endeavoring to identify, was a marked feature in the sketch I had shown him.

"Will you take a seat near by while I make a study of this matter?"

I turned with alacrity to obey. There was something in his air and manner which made me almost buoyant. Had my fanciful interpretation of what I had seen reached him with the conviction it had me? If so, there was hope,—hope for the man I loved, who had gone in and out between curtains, and not through any arch such as he had mentioned or I had described. Providence was working for me. I saw it in the way the men now moved about, swinging the window to and fro, under the instruction of the inspector, manipulating the lights, opening doors and drawing back curtains. Providence was working for me, and when, a few minutes later, I was asked to reseat myself in my old place at the supper-table and take another look in that slightly deflected glass, I knew that my effort had met with its reward, and that for the second time I was to receive the impression of a place now indelibly imprinted on my consciousness.

"Is not that it?" asked the inspector, pointing at the glass with a last look at the imperfect sketch I had made him, and which he still held in his hand.

"Yes," I eagerly responded. "All but the man. He whose figure I see there is another person entirely; I see no remorse, or even fear, in his looks."

"Of course not. You are looking at the reflection of one of my men. Miss Van Arsdale, do you recognize the place now under your eye?"

"I do not. You spoke of an arch in the hall, at the left of the carriage entrance, and I see an arch in the window-pane before me, but—"

"You are looking straight through the alcove,—perhaps you did not know that another door opened at its back,—into the passage which runs behind it. Farther on is the arch, and beyond that arch the side hall and staircase leading to the dressing-rooms. This door, the one in the rear of the alcove, I mean, is hidden from those entering from the main hall by draperies which have been hung over it for this occasion, but it is quite visible from the back passageway, and there can be no doubt that it was by its means the man, whose reflected image you saw, both entered and left the alcove. It is an important fact to establish, and we feel very much obliged to you for the aid you have given us in this matter."

Then, as I continued to stare at him in my elation and surprise, he added, in quick explanation:

"The lights in the alcove, and in the several parlors, are all hung with shades, as you must perceive, but the one in the hall, beyond the arch, is very bright, which accounts for the distinctness of this double reflection. Another thing,— and it is a very interesting point,—it would have been impossible for this reflection to be noticeable from where you sit, if the level of the alcove flooring had not been considerably higher than that of the main floor. But for this freak of the architect, the continual passing to and fro of people would have prevented the reflection in its passage from surface to surface. Miss Van Arsdale, it would seem that by one of those chances which happen but once or twice in a lifetime, every condition was propitious at the moment to make this reflection a possible occurrence, even the location and width of the several doorways and the exact point at which the portiere was drawn aside from the entrance to the alcove."

"It is wonderful," I cried, "wonderful!" Then, to his astonishment, perhaps, I asked if there was not a small door of communication between the passageway back of the alcove and the large central hall.

"Yes," he replied. "It opens just beyond the fireplace. Three small steps lead to it."

"I thought so," I murmured, but more to myself than to him. In my mind I was thinking how a man, if he so wished, could pass from the very heart of this assemblage into the quiet passageway, and so on into the alcove, without attracting very much attention from his fellow guests. I forgot that there was another way of approach even less noticeable that by the small staircase running up beyond the arch directly to the dressing-rooms.

That no confusion may arise in any one's mind in regard to these curious approaches, I subjoin a plan of this portion of the lower floor as it afterward appeared in the leading dailies.

"And Mr. Durand?" I stammered, as I followed the inspector back to the room where we had left that gentleman. "You will believe his statement now and look for this second intruder with the guiltily-hanging head and frightened mien?"

"Yes," he replied, stopping me on the threshold of the door and taking my hand kindly in his, "if—(don't start, my dear; life is full of trouble for young and old, and youth is the best time to face a sad experience) if he is not himself the man you saw staring in frightened horror at his breast. Have you not noticed that he is not dressed in all respects like the other gentlemen present? That, though he has not donned his overcoat, he has put on, somewhat prematurely, one might say, the large silk handkerchief lie presumably wears under it? Have you not noticed this, and asked yourself why?"

I had noticed it. I had noticed it from the moment I recovered from my fainting fit, but I had not thought it a matter of sufficient interest to ask, even of myself, his reason for thus hiding his shirt-front. Now I could not. My faculties were too confused, my heart too deeply shaken by the suggestion which the inspector's words conveyed, for me to be conscious of anything but the devouring question as to what I should do if, by my own mistaken zeal, I had succeeded in plunging the man I loved yet deeper into the toils in which he had become enmeshed.

The inspector left me no time for the settlement of this question. Ushering me back into the room where Mr. Durand and my uncle awaited our return in apparently unrelieved silence, he closed the door upon the curious eyes of the various persons still lingering in the hall, and abruptly said to Mr. Durand:

"The explanations you have been pleased to give of the manner in which this diamond came into your possession are not too fanciful for credence, if you can satisfy us on another point which has awakened some doubt in the mind of one of my men. Mr. Durand, you appear to have prepared yourself for departure somewhat prematurely. Do you mind removing that handkerchief for a moment? My reason for so peculiar a request will presently appear."

Alas, for my last fond hope! Mr. Durand, with a face as white as the background of snow framed by the uncurtained window against which he leaned, lifted his hand as if to comply with the inspector's request, then let it fall again with a grating laugh.

"I see that I am not likely to escape any of the results of my imprudence," he cried, and with a quick jerk bared his shirt-front.

A splash of red defiled its otherwise uniform whiteness! That it was the red of heart's blood was proved by the shrinking look he unconsciously cast at it.

IV. EXPLANATIONS

My love for Anson Durand died at sight of that crimson splash or I thought it did. In this spot of blood on the breast of him to whom I had given my heart I could read but one word—guilt—heinous guilt, guilt denied and now brought to light in language that could be seen and read by all men. Why should I stay in such a presence? Had not the inspector himself advised me to go?

Yes, but another voice bade me remain. Just as I reached the door, Anson Durand found his voice and I heard, in the full, sweet tones I loved so well:

"Wait I am not to be judged like this. I will explain!"

But here the inspector interposed.

"Do you think it wise to make any such attempt without the advice of counsel, Mr. Durand?"

The indignation with which Mr. Durand wheeled toward him raised in me a faint hope.

"Good God, yes!" he cried. "Would you have me leave Miss Van Arsdale one minute longer than is necessary to such dreadful doubts? Rita—Miss Van Arsdale—weakness, and weakness only, has brought me into my present position. I did not kill Mrs. Fairbrother, nor did I knowingly take her diamond, though appearances look that way, as I am very ready to acknowledge. I did go to her in the alcove, not once, but twice, and these are my reasons for doing so: About three months ago a certain well-known man of enormous wealth came to me with the request that I should procure for him a diamond of superior beauty. He wished to give it to his wife, and he wished it to outshine any which could now be found in New York. This meant sending abroad—an expense he was quite willing to incur on the sole condition that the stone should not disappoint him when he saw it, and that it was to be in his hands on the eighteenth of March, his wife's birthday. Never before had I had such an opportunity for a large stroke of business. Naturally elated, I entered at once into correspondence with the best known dealers on the other side, and last week a diamond was delivered to me which seemed to fill all the necessary requirements. I had never seen a finer stone, and was consequently rejoicing in my success, when some one, I do not remember who now, chanced to speak in my hearing of the wonderful stone possessed by a certain Mrs. Fairbrother—a stone so large, so brilliant and so precious altogether that she seldom wore it, though it was known to connoisseurs and had a great reputation at Tiffany's, where it had once been sent for some alteration in the setting. Was this stone larger and finer than the one I had procured with so much trouble? If so, my labor had all been in vain, for my patron must have known of this diamond and would expect to see it surpassed.

"I was so upset by this possibility that I resolved to see the jewel and make comparisons for myself. I found a friend who agreed to introduce me to the lady. She received me very graciously and was amiable enough until the subject of diamonds was broached, when she immediately stiffened and left me without an opportunity of proffering my request. However, on every other subject she was affable, and I found it easy enough to pursue the acquaintance till we were almost on friendly terms. But I never saw the diamond, nor would she talk about it, though I caused her some surprise when one day I drew out before her eyes the one I had procured for my patron and made her look at it. 'Fine,' she cried, 'fine!' But I failed to detect any envy in her manner, and so knew that I had not achieved the object set me by my wealthy customer. This was a woeful disappointment; yet, as Mrs. Fairbrother never wore her diamond, it was among the possibilities that he might be satisfied with the very fine gem I had obtained for him, and, influenced by this hope, I sent him this morning a request to come and see it tomorrow. Tonight I attended this ball, and almost as soon as I enter the drawing-room I hear that Mrs. Fairbrother is present and is wearing her famous jewel. What could you expect of me? Why, that I would make an effort to see it and so be ready with a reply to my exacting customer when he should ask me to-morrow if the stone I showed him had its peer in the city. But was not in the drawing-room then, and later I became interested elsewhere"—here he cast a look at me—"so that half the evening passed before I had an opportunity to join her in the so-called alcove, where I had seen her set up her miniature court. What passed between us in the short interview we held together you will find me prepared to state, if necessary. It was chiefly marked by the one short view I succeeded in obtaining of her marvelous diamond, in spite of the pains she took to hide it from me by some natural movement whenever she caught my eyes leaving her face. But in that one short look I had seen enough. This was a gem for a collector, not to be worn save in a royal presence. How had she come by it? And could Mr. Smythe expect me to procure him a stone like that? In my confusion I arose to depart, but the lady showed a disposition to keep me, and began chatting so vivaciously that I scarcely noticed that she was all the time engaged in drawing off her gloves. Indeed, I almost forgot the jewel, possibly because her movements hid it so completely, and only remembered it when, with a sudden turn from the window where she had drawn me to watch the falling flakes, she pressed the gloves into my hand with the coquettish request that I should take care of them for her. I remember, as I took them, of striving to catch another glimpse of the stone, whose brilliancy had dazzled me, but she had opened her fan between us. A moment after, thinking I heard approaching steps, I quitted the room. This was my first visit."

As he stopped, possibly for breath, possibly to judge to what extent I was impressed by his account, the inspector seized the opportunity to ask if Mrs. Fairbrother had been standing any of this time with her back to him. To which he answered yes, while they were in the window.

"Long enough for her to pluck off the jewel and thrust it into the gloves, if she had so wished?"

"Quite long enough."

"But you did not see her do this?"

"I did not."

"And so took the gloves without suspicion?"

"Entirely so."

"And carried them away?"

"Unfortunately, yes."

"Without thinking that she might want them the next minute?"

"I doubt if I was thinking seriously of her at all. My thoughts were on my own disappointment."

"Did you carry these gloves out in your hand?"

"No, in my pocket."

"I see. And you met—"

"No one. The sound I heard must have come from the rear hall."

"And there was nobody on the steps?"

"No. A gentleman was standing at their foot—Mr. Grey, the Englishman— but his face was turned another way, and he looked as if he had been in that same position for several minutes."

"Did this gentleman—Mr. Grey—see you?"

"I can not say, but I doubt it. He appeared to be in a sort of dream. There were other people about, but nobody with whom I was acquainted."

"Very good. Now for the second visit you acknowledge having paid this unfortunate lady."

The inspector's voice was hard. I clung a little more tightly to my uncle, and Mr. Durand, after one agonizing glance my way, drew himself up as if quite conscious that he had entered upon the most serious part of the struggle.

"I had forgotten the gloves in my hurried departure; but presently I remembered them, and grew very uneasy. I did not like carrying this woman's property about with me. I had engaged myself, an hour before, to Miss Van Arsdale, and was very anxious to rejoin her. The gloves worried me, and finally, after a little aimless wandering through the various rooms, I determined to go back and restore them to their owner. The doors of the supper-room had just been flung open, and the end of the hall near the alcove was comparatively empty, save for a certain quizzical friend of mine, whom I saw sitting with his partner on the yellow divan. I did not want to encounter him just then, for he had already joked me about my admiration for the lady with the diamond, and so I conceived the idea of approaching her by means of a second entrance to the alcove, unsuspected by most of those present, but perfectly well-known to me, who have been a frequent guest in this house. A door, covered by temporary draperies, connects, as you may know, this alcove with a passageway communicating directly with the hall of entrance and the up-stairs dressing-rooms. To go up the main stairs and come down by the side one, and so on, through a small archway, was a very simple matter for me. If no early-departing or late arriving guests were in that hall, I need fear but one encounter, and that was with the servant stationed at the carriage entrance. But even he was absent at this propitious instant, and I reached the door I sought without any unpleasantness. This door opened out instead of in,—this I also knew when planning this surreptitious intrusion, but, after pulling it open and reaching for the curtain, which hung completely across it, I found it not so easy to proceed as I had imagined. The stealthiness of my action held back my hand; then the faint sounds I heard within advised me that she was not alone, and that she might very readily regard with displeasure my unexpected entrance by a door of which she was possibly ignorant. I tell you all this because, if by any chance I was seen hesitating in face of that curtain, doubts might have been raised which I am anxious to dispel." Here his eyes left my face for that of the inspector.

"It certainly had a bad look,—that I don't deny; but I did not think of appearances then. I was too anxious to complete a task which had suddenly presented unexpected difficulties. That I listened before entering was very natural, and when I heard no voice, only something like a great sigh, I ventured to lift the curtain and step in. She was sitting, not where I had left her, but on a couch at the left of the usual entrance, her face toward me, and—you know how, Inspector. It was her last sigh I had heard. Horrified, for I had never looked on death before, much less crime, I reeled forward, meaning, I presume, to rush down the steps shouting for help, when, suddenly, something fell splashing on my shirt-front, and I saw myself marked with a stain of blood. This both frightened and bewildered me, and it was a minute or two before I had the courage to look up. When I did do so, I saw whence this drop had come. Not from her, though the red stream was pouring down the rich folds of her dress, but from a sharp needle-like instrument which had been thrust, point downward, in the open work of an antique lantern hanging near the doorway. What had happened to me might have happened to any one who chanced to be in that spot at that special moment, but I did not realize this then. Covering the splash with my hands, I edged myself back to the door by which I had entered, watching those deathful eyes and crushing under my feet the remnants of some broken china with which the carpet was bestrewn. I had no thought of her, hardly any of myself. To cross the room was all; to escape as secretly as I came, before the portiere so nearly drawn between me and the main hall should stir under the hand of some curious person entering. It was my first sight of blood; my first contact with crime, and that was what I did,—I fled."

The last word was uttered with a gasp. Evidently he was greatly affected by this horrible experience.

"I am ashamed of myself," he muttered, "but nothing can now undo the fact. I slid from the presence of this murdered woman as though she had been the victim of my own rage or cupidity; and, being fortunate enough to reach the dressing-room before the alarm had spread beyond the immediate vicinity of the alcove, found and put on the handkerchief, which made it possible for me to rush down and find Miss Van Arsdale, who, somebody told me, had fainted. Not till I stood over her in that remote corner beyond the supper-room did I again think of the gloves. What I did when I happened to think of them, you already know. I could have shown no greater cowardice if I had known that the murdered woman's diamond was hidden inside them. Yet, I did not know this, or even suspect it. Nor do I understand, now, her reason for placing it there. Why should Mrs. Fairbrother risk such an invaluable gem to the custody of one she knew so little? An unconscious custody, too? Was she afraid of being murdered if she retained this jewel?"

The inspector thought a moment, and then said:

"You mention your dread of some one entering by the one door before you could escape by the other. Do you refer to the friend you left sitting on the divan opposite?"

"No, my friend had left that seat. The portiere was sufficiently drawn for me to detect that. If I had waited a minute longer," he bitterly added, "I should have found my way open to the regular entrance, and so escaped all this."

"Mr. Durand, you are not obliged to answer any of my questions; but, if you wish, you may tell me whether, at this moment of apprehension, you thought of the danger you ran of being seen from outside by some one of the many coachmen passing by on the driveway?"

"No,—I did not even think of the window,—I don't know why; but, if any one passing by did see me, I hope they saw enough to substantiate my story."

The inspector made no reply. He seemed to be thinking. I heard afterward that the curtains, looped back in the early evening, had been found hanging at full length over this window by those who first rushed in upon the scene of death. Had he hoped to entrap Mr. Durand into some damaging admission? Or was he merely testing his truth? His expression afforded no clue to his thoughts, and Mr. Durand, noting this, remarked with some dignity:

"I do not expect strangers to accept these explanations, which must sound strange and inadequate in face of the proof I carry of having been with that woman after the fatal weapon struck her heart. But, to one who knows me, and knows me well, I can surely appeal for credence to a tale which I here declare to be as true as if I had sworn to it in a court of justice."

"Anson!" I passionately cried out, loosening my clutch upon my uncle's arm. My confidence in him had returned.

And then, as I noted the inspector's businesslike air, and my uncle's wavering look and unconvinced manner, I felt my heart swell, and, flinging all discretion to the wind, I bounded eagerly forward. Laying my hands in those of Mr. Durand, I cried fervently:

"I believe in you. Nothing but your own words shall ever shake my confidence in your innocence."

The sweet, glad look I received was my best reply. I could leave the room, after that.

But not the house. Another experience awaited me, awaited us all, before this full, eventful evening came to a close.

V. SUPERSTITION

I had gone up stairs for my wraps—my uncle having insisted on my withdrawing from a scene where my very presence seemed in some degree to compromise me.

Soon prepared for my departure, I was crossing the hall to the small door communicating with the side staircase where my uncle had promised to await me, when I felt myself seized by a desire to have another look below before leaving the place in which were centered all my deepest interests.

A wide landing, breaking up the main flight of stairs some few feet from the top, offered me an admirable point of view. With but little thought of possible consequences, and no thought at all of my poor, patient uncle, I slipped down to this landing, and, protected by the unusual height of its balustrade, allowed myself a parting glance at the scene with which my most poignant memories were henceforth to be connected.

Before me lay the large square of the central hall. Opening out from this was the corridor leading to the front door, and incidentally to the library. As my glance ran down this corridor, I beheld, approaching from the room just mentioned, the tall figure of the Englishman.

He halted as he reached the main hall and stood gazing eagerly at a group of men and women clustered near the fireplace—a group on which I no sooner cast my own eye than my attention also became fixed.

The inspector had come from the room where I had left him with Mr. Durand and was showing to these people the extraordinary diamond, which he had just recovered under such remarkable if not suspicious circumstances. Young heads and old were meeting over it, and I was straining my ears to hear such comments as were audible above the general hubbub, when Mr. Grey made a quick move and I looked his way again in time to mark his air of concern and the uncertainty he showed whether to advance or retreat.

Unconscious of my watchful eye, and noting, no doubt, that most of the persons in the group on which his own eye was leveled stood with their backs toward him, he made no effort to disguise his profound interest in the stone. His eye followed its passage from hand to hand with a covetous eagerness of which he may not have been aware, and I was not at all surprised when, after a short interval of troubled indecision, he impulsively stepped forward and begged the privilege of handling the gem himself.

Our host, who stood not far from the inspector, said something to that gentleman which led to this request being complied with. The stone was passed over to Mr. Grey, and I saw, possibly because my heart was in my eyes, that the great man's hand trembled as it touched his palm. Indeed, his whole frame trembled, and I was looking eagerly for the result of his inspection when, on his turning to hold the jewel up to the light, something happened so abnormal and so strange that no one who was fortunate (or unfortunate) enough to be present in the house at that instant will ever forget it.

This something was a cry, coming from no one knew where, which, unearthly in its shrillness and the power it had on the imagination, reverberated through the house and died away in a wail so weird, so thrilling and so prolonged that it gripped not only my own nerveless and weakened heart, but those of the ten strong men congregated below me. The diamond dropped from Mr. Grey's hand, and neither he nor any one else moved to pick it up. Not till silence had come again—a silence almost as unendurable to the sensitive ear as the cry which had preceded it—did any one stir or think of the gem. Then one gentleman after another bent to look for it, but with no success, till one of the waiters, who possibly had followed it with his eye or caught sight of its sparkle on the edge of the rug, whither it had rolled, sprang and picked it up and handed it back to Mr. Grey.

Instinctively the Englishman's hand closed on it, but it was very evident to me, and I think to all, that his interest in it was gone. If he looked at it he did not see it, for he stood like one stunned all the time that agitated men and women were running hither and thither in unavailing efforts to locate the sound yet ringing in their ears. Not till these various searchers had all come together again, in terror of a mystery they could not solve, did he let his hand fall and himself awake to the scene about him.

The words he at once gave utterance to were as remarkable as all the rest.

"Gentlemen," said he, "you must pardon my agitation. This cry—you need not seek its source—is one to which I am only too well accustomed. I have been the happy father of six children. Five I have buried, and, before the death of each, this same cry has echoed in my ears. I have but one child left, a daughter,—she is ill at the hotel. Do you wonder that I shrink from this note of warning, and show myself something less than a man under its influence? I am going home; but, first, one word about this stone." Here he lifted it and bestowed, or appeared to bestow on it, an anxious scrutiny, putting on his glasses and examining it carefully before passing it back to the inspector.

"I have heard," said he, with a change of tone which must have been noticeable to every one, "that this stone was a very superior one, and quite worthy of the fame it bore here in America. But, gentlemen, you have all been greatly deceived in it; no one more than he who was willing to commit murder for its possession. The stone, which you have just been good enough to allow me to inspect, is no diamond, but a carefully manufactured bit of paste not worth the rich and elaborate setting which has been given to it. I am sorry to be the one to say this, but I have made a study of precious stones, and I can not let this bare-faced imitation pass through my hands without a protest. Mr. Ramsdell," this to our host, "I beg you will allow me to utter my excuses, and depart at once. My daughter is worse,—this I know, as certainly as that I am standing here. The cry you have heard is the one superstition of our family. Pray God that I find her alive!"

After this, what could be said? Though no one who had heard him, not even my own romantic self, showed any belief in this interpretation of the remarkable sound that had just gone thrilling through the house, yet, in face of his declared acceptance of it as a warning, and the fact that all efforts had failed to locate the sound, or even to determine its source, no other course seemed open but to let this distinguished man depart with the suddenness his superstitious fears demanded.

That this was in opposition to the inspector's wishes was evident enough. Naturally, he would have preferred Mr. Grey to remain, if only to make clear his surprising conclusions in regard to a diamond which had passed through the hands of some of the best judges in the country, without a doubt having been raised as to its genuineness.

With his departure the inspector's manner changed. He glanced at the stone in his hand, and slowly shook his head.

"I doubt if Mr. Grey's judgment can be depended on, to-night," said he, and pocketed the gem as carefully as if his belief in its real value had been but little disturbed by the assertions of this renowned foreigner.

I have no distinct remembrance of how I finally left the house, or of what passed between my uncle and myself on our way home. I was numb with the shock, and neither my intelligence nor my feelings were any longer active. I recall but one impression, and that was the effect made on me by my old home on our arrival there, as of something new and strange; so much had happened, and such changes had taken place in myself since leaving it five hours before. But nothing else is vivid in my remembrance till that early hour of the dreary morning, when, on waking to the world with a cry, I beheld my uncle's anxious figure, bending over me from the foot-board.

Instantly I found tongue, and question after question leaped from my lips. He did not answer them; he could not; but when I grew feverish and insistent, he drew the morning paper from behind his back, and laid it quietly down within my reach. I felt calmed in an instant, and when, after a few affectionate words, he left me to myself, I seized on the sheet and read what so many others were reading at that moment throughout the city.

I spare you the account so far as it coincides with what I had myself seen and heard the night before. A few particulars which had not reached my ears will interest you. The instrument of death found in the place designated by Mr. Durand was one of note to such as had any taste or knowledge of curios. It was a stiletto of the most delicate type, long, keen and slender. Not an American product, not even of this century's manufacture, but a relic of the days when deadly thrusts were given in the corners and by-ways of medieval streets.

This made the first mystery.

The second was the as yet unexplainable presence, on the alcove floor, of two broken coffee-cups, which no waiter nor any other person, in fact, admitted having carried there. The tray, which had fallen from Peter Mooney's hand,—the waiter who had been the first to give the alarm of murder,—had held no cups, only ices. This was a fact, proved. But the handles of two cups had been found among the debris,—cups which must have been full, from the size of the coffee stain left on the rug where they had fallen.

In reading this I remembered that Mr. Durand had mentioned stepping on some broken pieces of china in his escape from the fatal scene, and, struck with this confirmation of a theory which was slowly taking form in my own mind, I passed on to the next paragraph, with a sense of expectation.

The result was a surprise. Others may have been told, I was not, that Mrs. Fairbrother had received a communication from outside only a few minutes previous to her death. A Mr. Fullerton, who had preceded Mr. Durand in his visit to the alcove, owned to having opened the window for her at some call or signal from outside, and taken in a small piece of paper which he saw lifted up from below on the end of a whip handle. He could not see who held the whip, but at Mrs. Fairbrother's entreaty he unpinned the note and gave it to her. While she was puzzling over it, for it was apparently far from legible, he took another look out in time to mark a figure rush from below toward the carriage drive. He did not recognize the figure nor would he know it again. As to the nature of the communication itself he could say nothing, save that Mrs. Fairbrother did not seem to be affected favorably by it. She frowned and was looking very gloomy when he left the alcove. Asked if he had pulled the curtains together after closing the window, he said that he had not; that she had not requested him to do so.

This story, which was certainly a strange one, had been confirmed by the testimony of the coachman who had lent his whip for the purpose. This coachman, who was known to be a man of extreme good nature, had seen no harm in lending his whip to a poor devil who wished to give a telegram or some such hasty message to the lady sitting just above them in a lighted window. The wind was fierce and the snow blinding, and it was natural that the man should duck his head, but he remembered his appearance well enough to say that he was either very cold or very much done up and that he wore a greatcoat with the collar pulled up about his ears. When he came back with the whip he seemed more cheerful than when he asked for it, but had no "thank you" for the favor done him, or if he had, it was lost in his throat and the piercing gale.

The communication, which was regarded by the police as a matter of the highest importance, had been found in her hand by the coroner. It was a mere scrawl written in pencil on a small scrap of paper. The following facsimile of the scrawl was given to the public in the hope that some one would recognize the handwriting.

The first two lines overlapped and were confused, but the last one was clear enough. Expect trouble if—If what? Hundreds were asking the question and at this very moment. I should soon be asking it, too, but first, I must make an effort to understand the situation,—a situation which up to now appeared to involve Mr. Durand, and Mr. Durand only, as the suspected party.

This was no more than I expected, yet it came with a shock under the broad glare of this wintry morning; so impossible did it seem in the light of every-day life that guilt could be associated in any one's mind with a man of such unblemished record and excellent standing. But the evidence adduced against him was of a kind to appeal to the common mind—we all know that evidence—

nor could I say, after reading the full account, that I was myself unaffected by its seeming weight. Not that my faith in his innocence was shaken. I had met his look of love and tender gratitude and my confidence in him had been restored, but I saw, with all the clearness of a mind trained by continuous study, how difficult it was going to be to counteract the prejudice induced, first, by his own inconsiderate acts, especially by that unfortunate attempt of his to secrete Mrs. Fairbrother's gloves in another woman's bag, and secondly, by his peculiar explanations—explanations which to many must seem forced and unnatural.

I saw and felt nerved to a superhuman task. I believed him innocent, and if others failed to prove him so, I would undertake to clear him myself,—I, the little Rita, with no experience of law or courts or crime, but with simply an unbounded faith in the man suspected and in the keenness of my own insight,— an insight which had already served me so well and would serve me yet better, once I had mastered the details which must be the prelude to all intelligent action.

The morning's report stopped with the explanations given by Mr. Durand of the appearances against him. Consequently no word appeared of the after events which had made such an impression at the time on all the persons present. Mr. Grey was mentioned, but simply as one of the guests, and to no one reading this early morning issue would any doubt come as to the genuineness of the diamond which, to all appearance, had been the leading motive in the commission of this great crime.

The effect on my own mind of this suppression was a curious one. I began to wonder if the whole event had not been a chimera of my disturbed brain—a nightmare which had visited me, and me alone, and not a fact to be reckoned with. But a moment's further thought served to clear my mind of all such doubts, and I perceived that the police had only exercised common prudence in withholding Mr. Grey's sensational opinion of the stone till it could be verified by experts.

The two columns of gossip devoted to the family differences which had led to the separation of Mr. and Mrs. Fairbrother, I shall compress into a few lines. They had been married three years before in the city of Baltimore. He was a rich man then, but not the multimillionaire he is to-day. Plain-featured and without manner, lie was no mate for this sparkling coquette, whose charm was of the kind which grows with exercise. Though no actual scandal was ever associated with her name, he grew tired of her caprices, and the conquests which she made no endeavor to hide either from him or from the world at large; and at some time during the previous year they had come to a friendly understanding which led to their living apart, each in grand style and with a certain deference to the proprieties which retained them their friends and an enviable place in society. He was not often invited where she was, and she never appeared in any assemblage where he was expected; but with this exception, little feeling was shown; matters progressed smoothly, and to their credit, let it be said, no one ever heard either of them speak otherwise than considerately of the other. He was at present out or town, having started some three weeks before for the southwest, but would probably return on receipt of the telegram which had been sent him.

The comments made on the murder were necessarily hurried. It was called a mystery, but it was evident enough that Mr. Durand's detention was looked on as the almost certain prelude to his arrest on the charge of murder.

I had had some discipline in life. Although a favorite of my wealthy uncle, I had given up very early the prospects he held out to me of a continued enjoyment of his bounty, and entered on duties which required self-denial and hard work. I did this because I enjoy having both my mind and heart occupied. To be necessary to some one, as a nurse is to a patient, seemed to me an enviable fate till I came under the influence of Anson Durand. Then the craving of all women for the common lot of their sex became my craving also; a craving, however, to which I failed at first to yield, for I felt that it was unshared, and thus a token of weakness. Fighting my battle, I succeeded in winning it, as I thought, just as the nurse's diploma was put in my hands. Then came the great surprise of my life. Anson Durand expressed his love for me and I awoke to the fact that all my preparation had been for home joys and a woman's true existence. One hour of ecstasy in the light of this new hope, then tragedy and something approaching chaos! Truly I had been through a schooling. But was it one to make me useful in the only way I could be useful now? I did not know; I did not care; I was determined on my course, fit or unfit, and, in the relief brought by this appeal to my energy, I rose and dressed and went about the duties of the day.

One of these was to determine whether Mr. Grey, on his return to his hotel, had found his daughter as ill as his fears had foreboded. A telephone message or two satisfied me on this point. Miss Grey was very ill, but not considered dangerously so; indeed, if anything, her condition was improved, and if nothing happened in the way of fresh complications, the prospects were that she would be out in a fortnight.

I was not surprised. It was more than I had expected. The cry of the banshee in an American house was past belief, even in an atmosphere surcharged with fear and all the horror surrounding a great crime; and in the secret reckoning I was making against a person I will not even name at this juncture, I added it as another suspicious circumstance.

VI. SUSPENSE

To relate the full experiences of the next few days would be to encumber my narrative with unnecessary detail.

I did not see Mr. Durand again. My uncle, so amenable in most matters, proved Inexorable on this point. Till Mr. Durand's good name should be restored by the coroner's verdict, or such evidence brought to light as should effectually place him beyond all suspicion, I was to hold no communication with him of any sort whatever. I remember the very words with which my uncle ended the one exhaustive conversation we had on the subject. They were these:

"You have fully expressed to Mr. Durand your entire confidence In his Innocence. That must suffice him for the present. If he Is the honest gentleman you think him, It will."

As uncle seldom asserted himself, and as he is very much in earnest when he does, I made no attempt to combat this resolution, especially as it met the approval of my better judgment. But though my power to convey sympathy fell thus under a yoke, my thoughts and feelings remained free, and these were all consecrated to the man struggling under an imputation, the disgrace and humiliation of which he was but poorly prepared, by his former easy life of social and business prosperity, to meet.

For Mr. Durand, in spite of the few facts which came up from time to time in confirmation of his story, continued to be almost universally regarded as a suspect.

This seemed to me very unjust. What if no other clue offered—no other clue, I mean, recognized as such by police or public! Was he not to have the benefit of whatever threw a doubt on his own culpability? For instance, that splash of blood on his shirt-front, which I had seen, and the shape of which I knew! Why did not the fact that it was a splash and not a spatter (and spatter it would have been had it spurted there, instead of falling from above, as he stated), count for more in the minds of those whose business it was to probe into the very heart of this crime? To me, it told such a tale of innocence that I wondered how a man like the inspector could pass over it. But later I understood. A single word enlightened me. The stain, it was true, was In the form of a splash and not a spurt, but a splash would have been the result of a drop falling from the reeking end of the stiletto, whether it dislodged itself early or late. And what was there to prove that this drop had not fallen at the instant the stiletto was being thrust Into the lantern, instead of after the escape of the criminal, and the entrance of another man?

But the mystery of the broken coffee-cups! For that no explanation seemed to be forthcoming.

And the still unsolved one of the written warning found in the murdered woman's hand—a warning which had been deciphered to read: "Be warned! He means to be at the ball! Expect trouble if—" Was that to be looked upon as directed against a man who, from the nature of his projected attempt, would take no one into his confidence?

Then the stiletto—a photographic reproduction of which was in all the papers—was that the kind of instrument which a plain New York gentleman would be likely to use In a crime of this nature? It was a marked and unique article, capable, as one would think, of being easily traced to its owner. Had it been claimed by Mr. Ramsdell, had it been recognized as one of the many works of art scattered about the highly-decorated alcove, its employment as a means of death would have gone only to prove the possibly unpremeditated nature of the crime, and so been valueless as the basis of an argument in favor of Mr. Durand's innocence. But Mr. Ramsdell had disclaimed from the first all knowledge of it, consequently one could but feel justified in asking whether a man of Mr. Durand's judgment would choose such an extraordinary weapon in meditating so startling a crime which from its nature and circumstance could not fail to attract the attention of the whole civilized world.

Another argument, advanced by himself and subscribed to by all his friends, was this: That a dealer in precious stones would be the last man to seek by any unlawful means to possess so conspicuous a jewel. For he, better than any one else, would know the impossibility of disposing of a gem of this distinction in any market short of the Orient. To which the unanswerable reply was made that no one attributed to him any such folly; that if he had planned to possess himself of this great diamond, it was for the purpose of eliminating it from competition with the one he had procured for Mr. Smythe; an argument, certainly, which drove us back on the only plea we had at our command—his hitherto unblemished reputation and the confidence which was felt In him by those who knew him.

But the one circumstance which affected me most at the time, and which undoubtedly was the source of the greatest confusion to all minds, whether official or otherwise, was the unexpected confirmation by experts of Mr. Grey's opinion in regard to the diamond. His name was not used, indeed it had been kept out of the papers with the greatest unanimity, but the hint he had given the inspector at Mr. Ramsdell's ball had been acted upon and, the proper tests having been made, the stone, for which so many believed a life to have been risked and another taken, was declared to be an imitation, fine and successful beyond all parallel, but still an imitation, of the great and renowned gem which had passed through Tiffany's hands a twelve-month before: a decision which fell like a thunderbolt on all such as had seen the diamond blazing in unapproachable brilliancy on the breast of the unhappy Mrs. Fairbrother only an hour or two before her death.

On me the effect was such that for days I lived in a dream, a condition that, nevertheless, did not prevent me from starting a certain little inquiry of my own, of which more hereafter.

Here let me say that I did not share the general confusion on this topic. I had my own theory, both as to the cause of this substitution and the moment when it was made. But the time had not yet come for me to advance it. I could only stand back and listen to the suppositions aired by the press, suppositions which fomented so much private discussion that ere long the one question most frequently heard in this connection was not who struck the blow which killed Mrs. Fairbrother (this was a question which some seemed to think settled), but whose juggling hand had palmed off the paste for the diamond, and how and when and where had the jugglery taken place?

Opinions on this point were, as I have said, many and various. Some fixed upon the moment of exchange as that very critical and hardly appreciable one elapsing between the murder and Mr. Durand's appearance upon the scene. This theory, I need not say, was advanced by such as believed that while he was not guilty of Mrs. Fairbrother's murder, lie had been guilty of taking advantage of the same to rob the body of what, in the terror and excitement of the moment, he evidently took to be her great gem. To others, among whom were many eyewitnesses of the event, it appeared to be a conceded fact that this substitution had been made prior to the ball and with Mrs. Fairbrother's full cognizance. The effectual way in which she had wielded her fan between the glittering ornament on her breast and the inquisitive glances constantly leveled upon it might at the time have been due to coquetry, but to them it looked much more like an expression of fear lest the deception in which she was indulging should be discovered. No one fixed the time where I did; but then, no one but myself had watched the scene with the eyes of love; besides, and this must be remembered, most people, among whom I ventured to count the police officials, were mainly interested in proving Mr. Durand guilty, while I, with contrary mind, was bent on establishing such facts as confirmed the explanations he had been pleased to give us, explanations which necessitated a conviction, on Mrs. Fairbrother's part, of the great value of the jewel she wore, and the consequent advisability of ridding herself of it temporarily, if, as so many believed, the full letter of the warning should read: "Be warned, he means to be at the ball. Expect trouble if you are found wearing the great diamond."

True, she may herself have been deceived concerning it. Unconsciously to herself, she may have been the victim of a daring fraud on the part of some hanger-on who had access to her jewels, but, as no such evidence had yet come to life, as she had no recognized, or, so far as could be learned, secret lover or dishonest dependent; and, moreover, as no gem of such unusual value was known to have been offered within the year, here or abroad, in public or private market, I could not bring myself to credit this assumption; possibly because I was so ignorant as to credit another, and a different one,—one which you have already seen growing in my mind, and which, presumptuous as it was, kept my courage from failing through all those dreadful days of enforced waiting and suspense. For I was determined not to intrude my suggestions, valuable as I considered them, till all hope was gone of his being righted by the judgment of those who would not lightly endure the interference of such an insignificant mote in the great scheme of justice as myself.

The inquest, which might be trusted to bring out all these doubtful points, had been delayed in anticipation of Mr. Fairbrother's return. His testimony could not but prove valuable, if not in fixing the criminal, at least in settling the moot point as to whether the stone, which the estranged wife had carried away with her on leaving the house, had been the genuine one returned to him from Tiffany's or the well-known imitation now in the hands of the police. He had been located somewhere in the mountains of lower Colorado, but, strange to say, It had been found impossible to enter into direct communication with him; nor was it known whether he was aware as yet of his wife's tragic death. So affairs went slowly in New York and the case seemed to come to a standstill, when public opinion was suddenly reawakened and a more definite turn given to the whole matter by a despatch from Santa Fe to the Associated Press. This despatch was to the effect that Abner Fairbrother had passed through that city some three days before on his way to his new mining camp, the Placide; that he then showed symptoms of pneumonia, and from advices since received might be regarded as a very sick man.

Ill,—well, that explained matters. His silence, which many had taken for indifference, was that of a man physically disabled and unfit for exertion of any kind. Ill,—a tragic circumstance which roused endless conjecture. Was he aware, or was he not aware, of his wife's death? Had he been taken ill before or after he left Colorado for New Mexico? Was he suffering mainly from shock, or, as would appear from his complaint, from a too rapid change of climate?

The whole country seethed with excitement, and my poor little unthought-of, insignificant self burned with impatience, which only those who have been subjected to a like suspense can properly estimate. Would the proceedings which were awaited with so much anxiety be further delayed? Would Mr. Durand remain indefinitely in durance and under such a cloud of disgrace as would kill some men and might kill him? Should I be called upon to endure still longer the suffering which this entailed upon me, when I thought I knew?

But fortune was less obdurate than I feared. Next morning a telegraphic statement from Santa Fe settled one of the points of this great dispute, a statement which you will find detailed at more length in the following communication, which appeared a few days later in one of our most enterprising journals.

It was from a resident correspondent in New Mexico, and was written, as the editor was careful to say, for his own eyes and not for the public. He had ventured, however, to give It in full, knowing the great interest which this whole subject had for his readers.

VII. NIGHT AND A VOICE

Not to be outdone by the editor, I insert the article here with all its details, the importance of which I trust I have anticipated.

SANTA FE, N.M., April—.

Arrived in Santa Fe, I inquired where Abner Fairbrother could be found. I was told that he was at his mine, sick.

Upon inquiring as to the location of the Placide, I was informed that it was fifteen miles or so distant in the mountains, and upon my expressing an intention of going there immediately, I was given what I thought very unnecessary advice and then directed to a certain livery stable, where I was told I could get the right kind of a horse and such equipment as I stood in need of.

I thought I was equipped all right as it was, but I said nothing and went on to the livery stable. Here I was shown a horse which I took to at once and was about to mount, when a pair of leggings was brought to me.

"You will need these for your journey," said the man.

"Journey!" I repeated. "Fifteen miles!"

The livery stable keeper—a half-breed with a peculiarly pleasant smile—cocked up his shoulders with the remark:

"Three men as willing but as inexperienced as yourself have attempted the same journey during the last week and they all came back before they reached the divide. You will probably come back, too; but I shall give you as fair a start as if I knew you were going straight through."

"But a woman has done it," said I; "a nurse from the hospital went up that very road last week."

"Oh, women! they can do anything—women who are nurses. But they don't start off alone. You are going alone."

"Yes," I remarked grimly. "Newspaper correspondents make their journeys singly when they can."

"Oh! you are a newspaper correspondent! Why do so many men from the papers want to see that sick old man? Because he's so rich?"

"Don't you know?" I asked.

He did not seem to.

I wondered at his ignorance but did not enlighten him.

"Follow the trail and ask your way from time to time. All the goatherds know where the Placide mine is."

Such were his simple instructions as he headed my horse toward the canyon. But as I drew off, he shouted out:

"If you get stuck, leave it to the horse. He knows more about it than you do."

With a vague gesture toward the northwest, he turned away, leaving me in contemplation of the grandest scenery I had yet come upon in all my travels.

Fifteen miles! but those miles lay through the very heart of the mountains, ranging anywhere from six to seven thousand feet high. In ten minutes the city and all signs of city life were out of sight. In five more I was seemingly as far removed from all civilization as if I had gone a hundred miles into the wilderness.

As my horse settled down to work, picking his way, now here and now there, sometimes over the brown earth, hard and baked as in a thousand furnaces, and sometimes over the stunted grass whose needle-like stalks seemed never to have known moisture, I let my eyes roam to such peaks as were not cut off from view by the nearer hillsides, and wondered whether the snow which capped them was whiter than any other or the blue of the sky bluer, that the two together had the effect upon me of cameo work on a huge and unapproachable scale.

Certainly the effect of these grand mountains, into which you leap without any preparation from the streets and market-places of America's oldest city, is such as is not easily described.

We struck water now and then,—narrow water—courses which my horse followed in mid stream, and, more interesting yet, goatherds with their flocks, Mexicans all, who seemed to understand no English, but were picturesque enough to look at and a welcome break in the extreme lonesomeness of the way.

I had been told that they would serve me as guides if I felt at all doubtful of the trail, and in one or two instances they proved to be of decided help. They could gesticulate, if they could not speak English, and when I tried them with the one word Placide they would nod and point out which of the many side canyons I was to follow. But they always looked up as they did so, up, up, till I took to looking up, too, and when, after miles multiplied indefinitely by the winding of the trail, I came out upon a ledge from which a full view of the opposite range could be had, and saw fronting me, from the side of one of its tremendous peaks, the gap of a vast hole not two hundred feet from the snowline, I knew that, inaccessible as it looked, I was gazing up at the opening of Abner Fairbrother's new mine, the Placide.

The experience was a strange one. The two ranges approached so nearly that it seemed as if a ball might be tossed from one to the other. But the chasm between was stupendous. I grew dizzy as I looked downward and saw the endless zigzags yet to be traversed step by step before the bottom of the canyon could be reached, and then the equally interminable zigzags up the acclivity beyond, all of which I must trace, still step by step, before I could hope to arrive at the camp which, from where I stood, looked to be almost within hail of my voice.

I have described the mine as a hole. That was all I saw at first—a great black hole in the dark brown earth of the mountain-side, from which ran down a still darker streak into the waste places far below it. But as I looked longer I saw that it was faced by a ledge cut out of the friable soil, on which I was now able to descry the pronounced white of two or three tent-tops and some other signs of life, encouraging enough to the eye of one whose lot it was to crawl like a fly up that tremendous mountain-side.

Truly I could understand why those three men, probably newspaper correspondents like myself, had turned back to Santa Fe, after a glance from my present outlook. But though I understood I did not mean to duplicate their retreat.

The sight of those tents, the thought of what one of them contained, inspired me with new courage, and, releasing my grip upon the rein, I allowed my patient horse to proceed. Shortly after this I passed the divide—that is where the water sheds both ways—then the descent began. It was zigzag, just as the climb had been, but I preferred the climb. I did not have the unfathomable spaces so constantly before me, nor was my imagination so active. It was fixed on heights to be attained rather than on valleys to roll into. However, I did not roll.

The Mexican saddle held me securely at whatever angle I was poised, and once the bottom was reached I found that I could face, with considerable equanimity, the corresponding ascent. Only, as I saw how steep the climb bade fair to be, I did not see how I was ever to come down again. Going up was possible, but the descent—

However, as what goes up must in the course of nature come down, I put this question aside and gave my horse his head, after encouraging him with a few blades of grass, which he seemed to find edible enough, though they had the look and something of the feel of spun glass.

How we got there you must ask this good animal, who took all the responsibility and did all the work. I merely clung and balanced, and at times, when he rounded the end of a zigzag, for instance, I even shut my eyes, though the prospect was magnificent. At last even his patience seemed to give out, and he stopped and trembled. But before I could open my eyes on the abyss beneath he made another effort. I felt the brush of tree branches across my face, and, looking up, saw before me the ledge or platform dotted with tents, at which I had looked with such longing from the opposite hillsides.

Simultaneously I heard voices, and saw approaching a bronzed and bearded man with strongly-marked Scotch features and a determined air.

"The doctor!" I involuntarily exclaimed, with a glance at the small and curious tent before which he stood guard.

"Yes, the doctor," he answered in unexpectedly good English. "And who are you? Have you brought the mail and those medicines I sent for?"

"No," I replied with as propitiatory a smile as I could muster up in face of his brusk forbidding expression. "I came on my own errand. I am a representative of the New York—and I hope you will not deny me a word with Mr. Fairbrother."

With a gesture I hardly knew how to interpret he took my horse by the rein and led us on a few steps toward another large tent, where he motioned me to descend. Then he laid his hand on my shoulder and, forcing me to meet his eye, said:

"You have made this journey—I believe you said from New York—to see Mr. Fairbrother. Why?"

"Because Mr. Fairbrother is at present the most sought-for man in America," I returned boldly. "His wife—you know about his wife—"

"No. How should I know about his wife? I know what his temperature is and what his respiration is—but his wife? What about his wife? He don't know anything about her now himself; he is not allowed to read letters."

"But you read the papers. You must have known, before you left Santa Fe, of Mrs. Fairbrother's foul and most mysterious murder in New York. It has been the theme of two continents for the last ten days."

He shrugged his shoulders, which might mean anything, and confined his reply to a repetition of my own words.

"Mrs. Fairbrother murdered!" he exclaimed, but in a suppressed voice, to which point was given by the cautious look he cast behind him at the tent which had drawn my attention. "He must not know it, man. I could not answer for his life if he received the least shock in his present critical condition. Murdered? When?"

"Ten days ago, at a ball in New York. It was after Mr. Fairbrother left the city. He was expected to return, after hearing the news, but he seems to have kept straight on to his destination. He was not very fond of his wife,—that is, they have not been living together for the last year. But he could not help feeling the shock of her death which he must have heard of somewhere along the route."

"He has said nothing in his delirium to show that he knew it. It is possible, just possible, that he didn't read the papers. He could not have been well for days before he reached Santa Fe."

"When were you called in to attend him?"

"The very night after he reached this place. It was thought he wouldn't live to reach the camp. But he is a man of great pluck. He held up till his foot touched this platform. Then he succumbed."

"If he was as sick as that," I muttered, "why did he leave Santa Fe? He must have known what it would mean to be sick here."

"I don't think he did. This is his first visit to the mine. He evidently knew nothing of the difficulties of the road. But he would not stop. He was determined to reach the camp, even after he had been given a sight of it from the opposite mountain. He told them that he had once crossed the Sierras in midwinter. But he wasn't a sick man then."

"Doctor, they don't know who killed his wife."

"He didn't."

"I know, but under such circumstances every fact bearing on the event is of immense importance. There is one which Mr. Fairbrother only can make clear. It can be said in a word—"

The grim doctor's eye flashed angrily and I stopped.

"Were you a detective from the district attorney's office in New York, sent on with special powers to examine him, I should still say what I am going to say now. While Mr. Fairbrother's temperature and pulse remain where they now are, no one shall see him and no one shall talk to him save myself and his nurse."

I turned with a sick look of disappointment toward the road up which I had so lately come. "Have I panted, sweltered, trembled, for three mortal hours on the worst trail a man ever traversed to go back with nothing for my journey? That seems to me hard lines. Where is the manager of this mine?"

The doctor pointed toward a man bending over the edge of the great hole from which, at that moment, a line of Mexicans was issuing, each with a sack on his back which he flung down before what looked like a furnace built of clay.

"That's he. Mr. Haines, of Philadelphia. What do you want of him?"

"Permission to stay the night. Mr. Fairbrother may be better to-morrow."

"I won't allow it and I am master here, so far as my patient is concerned. You couldn't stay here without talking, and talking makes excitement, and excitement is just what he can not stand. A week from now I will see about it— that is, if my patient continues to improve. I am not sure that he will."

"Let me spend that week here. I'll not talk any more than the dead. Maybe the manager will let me carry sacks."

"Look here," said the doctor, edging me farther and farther away from the tent he hardly let out of his sight for a moment. "You're a canny lad, and shall have your bite and something to drink before you take your way back. But back you go before sunset and with this message: No man from any paper north or south will be received here till I hang out a blue flag. I say blue, for that is the color of my bandana. When my patient is in a condition to discuss murder I'll hoist it from his tent-top. It can be seen from the divide, and if you want to camp there on the lookout, well and good. As for the police, that's another matter. I will see them if they come, but they need not expect to talk to my patient. You may say so down there. It will save scrambling up this trail to no purpose."

"You may count on me," said I; "trust a New York correspondent to do the right thing at the right time to head off the boys. But I doubt if they will believe me."

"In that case I shall have a barricade thrown up fifty feet down the mountain-side," said he.

"But the mail and your supplies?"

"Oh, the burros can make their way up. We shan't suffer."

"You are certainly master," I remarked.

All this time I had been using my eyes. There was not much to see, but what there was was romantically interesting. Aside from the furnace and what was going on there, there was little else but a sleeping-tent, a cooking-tent, and the small one I had come on first, which, without the least doubt, contained the sick man. This last tent was of a peculiar construction and showed the primitive nature of everything at this height. It consisted simply of a cloth thrown over a thing like a trapeze. This cloth did not even come to the ground on either side, but stopped short a foot or so from the flat mound of adobe which serves as a base or floor for hut or tent in New Mexico. The rear of the simple tent abutted on the mountain-side; the opening was toward the valley. I felt an intense desire to look into this opening,—so intense that I thought I would venture on an attempt to gratify it. Scrutinizing the resolute face of the man before me and flattering myself that I detected signs of humor underlying his professional bruskness, I asked, somewhat mournfully, if he would let me go away without so much as a glance at the man I had come so far to see. A glimpse would satisfy me I assured him, as the hint of a twinkle flashed in his eye. "Surely there will be no harm in that. I'll take it instead of supper."

He smiled, but not encouragingly, and I was feeling very despondent, indeed, when the canvas on which our eyes were fixed suddenly shook and the calm figure of a woman stepped out before us, clad in the simplest garb, but showing in every line of face and form a character of mingled kindness and shrewdness. She was evidently on the lookout for the doctor, for she made a sign as she saw him and returned instantly into the tent.

"Mr. Fairbrother has just fallen asleep," he explained. "It isn't discipline and I shall have to apologize to Miss Serra, but if you will promise not to speak nor make the least disturbance I will let you take the one peep you prefer to supper."

"I promise," said I.

Leading the way to the opening, he whispered a word to the nurse, then motioned me to look in. The sight was a simple one, but to me very impressive. The owner of palaces, a man to whom millions were as thousands to such poor devils as myself, lay on an improvised bed of evergreens, wrapped in a horse blanket and with nothing better than another of these rolled up under his head. At his side sat his nurse on what looked like the uneven stump of a tree. Close to her hand was a tolerably flat stone, on which I saw arranged a number of bottles and such other comforts as were absolutely necessary to a proper care of the sufferer.

That was all. In these few words I have told the whole story. To be sure, this simple tent, perched seven thousand feet and more above sea-level, had one advantage which even his great house in New York could not offer This was the out look. Lying as he did facing the valley, he had only to open his eyes to catch a full view of the panorama of sky and mountain stretched out before him. It was glorious; whether seen at morning, noon or night, glorious. But I doubt if he would not gladly have exchanged it for a sight of his home walls.

As I started to go, a stir took place in the blanket wrapped about his chin, and I caught a glimpse of the iron-gray head and hollow cheeks of the great financier. He was a very sick man. Even I could see that. Had I obtained the permission I sought and been allowed to ask him one of the many questions burning on my tongue, I should have received only delirium for reply. There was no reaching that clouded intelligence now, and I felt grateful to the doctor for convincing me of it.

I told him so and thanked him quite warmly when we were well away from the tent, and his answer was almost kindly, though he made no effort to hide his impatience and anxiety to see me go. The looks he cast at the sun were significant, and, having no wish to antagonize him and every wish to visit the spot again, I moved toward my horse with the intention of untying him.

To my surprise the doctor held me back.

"You can't go to-night," said he, "your horse has hurt himself."

It was true. There was something the matter with the animal's left forefoot. As the doctor lifted it, the manager came up. He agreed with the doctor. I could not make the descent to Santa Fe on that horse that night. Did I feel elated? Rather. I had no wish to descend. Yet I was far from foreseeing what the night was to bring me.

I was turned over to the manager, but not without a final injunction from the doctor. "Not a word to any one about your errand! Not a word about the New York tragedy, as you value Mr. Fairbrother's life."

"Not a word," said I.

Then he left me.

To see the sun go down and the moon come up from a ledge hung, as it were, in mid air! The experience was novel—but I refrain. I have more important matters to relate.

I was given a bunk at the extreme end of the long sleeping-tent, and turned in with the rest. I expected to sleep, but on finding that I could catch a sight of the sick tent from under the canvas, I experienced such fascination in watching this forbidden spot that midnight came before I had closed my eyes. Then all desire to sleep left me, for the patient began to moan and presently to talk, and, the stillness of the solitary height being something abnormal, I could sometimes catch the very words. Devoid as they were of all rational meaning, they excited my curiosity to the burning point; for who could tell if he might not say something bearing on the mystery?

But that fevered mind had recurred to early scenes and the babble which came to my ears was all of mining camps in the Rockies and the dicker of horses. Perhaps the uneasy movement of my horse pulling at the end of his tether had disturbed him. Perhaps—

But at the inner utterance of the second "perhaps" I found myself up on my elbow listening with all my ears, and staring with wide-stretched eyes at the thicket of stunted trees where the road debouched on the platform. Something was astir there besides my horse. I could catch sounds of an unmistakable nature. A rider was coming up the trail.

Slipping back into my place, I turned toward the doctor, who lay some two or three bunks nearer the opening. He had started up, too, and in a moment was out of the tent. I do not think he had observed my action, for it was very dark where I lay and his back had been turned toward me. As for the others, they slept like the dead, only they made more noise.

Interested—everything is interesting at such a height—I brought my eye to bear on the ledge, and soon saw by the limpid light of a full moon the stiff, short branches of the trees, on which my gaze was fixed, give way to an advancing horse and rider.

"Halloo!" saluted the doctor in a whisper, which was in itself a warning. "Easy there! We have sickness in this camp and it's a late hour for visitors."

"I know?"

The answer was subdued, but earnest.

50

"I'm the magistrate of this district. I've a question to ask this sick man, on behalf of the New York Chief of Police, who is a personal friend of mine. It is connected with—"

"Hush!"

The doctor had seized him by the arm and turned his face away from the sick tent. Then the two heads came together and an argument began.

I could not hear a word of it, but their motions were eloquent. My sympathy was with the magistrate, of course, and I watched eagerly while he passed a letter over to the doctor, who vainly strove to read it by the light of the moon. Finding this impossible, he was about to return it, when the other struck a match and lit a lantern hanging from the horn of his saddle. The two heads came together again, but as quickly separated with every appearance of irreconcilement, and I was settling back with sensations of great disappointment, when a sound fell on the night so unexpected to all concerned that with a common impulse each eye sought the sick tent.

"Water! will some one give me water?" a voice had cried, quietly and with none of the delirium which had hitherto rendered it unnatural.

The doctor started for the tent. There was the quickness of surprise in his movement and the gesture he made to the magistrate, as he passed in, reawakened an expectation in my breast which made me doubly watchful.

Providence was intervening in our favor, and I was not surprised to see him presently reissue with the nurse, whom he drew into the shadow of the trees, where they had a short conference. If she returned alone into the tent after this conference I should know that the matter was at an end and that the doctor had decided to maintain his authority against that of the magistrate. But she remained outside and the magistrate was invited to join their council; when they again left the shadow of the trees it was to approach the tent.

The magistrate, who was in the rear, could not have more than passed the opening, but I thought him far enough inside not to detect any movement on my part, so I took advantage of the situation to worm myself out of my corner and across the ledge to where the tent made a shadow in the moonlight.

Crouching close, and laying my ear against the canvas, I listened.

The nurse was speaking in a gently persuasive tone. I imagined her kneeling by the head of the patient and breathing words into his ear. These were what I heard:

"You love diamonds. I have often noticed that; you look so long at the ring on your hand. That is why I have let it stay there, though at times I have feared it would drop off and roll away over the adobe down the mountain-side. Was I right?"

"Yes, yes." The words came with difficulty, but they were clear enough. "It's of small value. I like it because—"

He appeared to be too weak to finish.

A pause, during which she seemed to edge nearer to him.

"We all have some pet keepsake," said she. "But I should never have supposed this stone of yours an inexpensive one. But I forget that you are the owner of a very large and remarkable diamond, a diamond that is spoken of sometimes in the papers. Of course, if you have a gem like that, this one must appear very small and valueless to you."

"Yes, this is nothing, nothing." And he appeared to turn away his head.

"Mr. Fairbrother! Pardon me, but I want to tell you something about that big diamond of yours. You have been in and have not been able to read your letters, so do not know that your wife has had some trouble with that diamond. People have said that it is not a real stone, but a well-executed imitation. May I write to her that this is a mistake, that it is all you have ever claimed for it—that is, an unusually large diamond of the first water?"

I listened in amazement. Surely, this was an insidious way to get at the truth,—a woman's way, but who would say it was not a wise one, the wisest, perhaps, which could be taken under the circumstances? What would his reply be? Would it show that he was as ignorant of his wife's death as was generally believed, both by those about him here and those who knew him well in New York? Or would the question convey nothing further to him than the doubt—in itself an insult of the genuineness of that great stone which had been his pride?

A murmur—that was all it could be called—broke from his fever-dried lips and died away in an inarticulate gasp. Then, suddenly, sharply, a cry broke from him, an intelligible cry, and we heard him say:

"No imitation! no imitation! It was a sun! a glory! No other like it! It lit the air! it blazed, it burned! I see it now! I see—"

There the passion succumbed, the strength failed; another murmur, another, and the great void of night which stretched over—I might almost say under us—was no more quiet or seemingly impenetrable than the silence of that moon-enveloped tent.

Would he speak again? I did not think so. Would she even try to make him? I did not think this, either. But I did not know the woman.

Softly her voice rose again. There was a dominating insistence in her tones, gentle as they were; the insistence of a healthy mind which seeks to control a weakened one.

"You do not know of any imitation, then? It was the real stone you gave her. You are sure of it; you would be ready to swear to it if—say just yes or no," she finished in gentle urgency.

Evidently he was sinking again into unconsciousness, and she was just holding him back long enough for the necessary word.

It came slowly and with a dragging intonation, but there was no mistaking the ring of truth with which he spoke.

"Yes," said he.

When I heard the doctor's voice and felt a movement in the canvas against which I leaned, I took the warning and stole back hurriedly to my quarters.

I was scarcely settled, when the same group of three I had before watched silhouetted itself again against the moonlight. There was some talk, a mingling and separating of shadows; then the nurse glided back to her duties and the two men went toward the clump of trees where the horse had been tethered.

Ten minutes and the doctor was back in his bunk. Was it imagination, or did I feel his hand on my shoulder before he finally lay down and composed himself to sleep? I can not say; I only know that I gave no sign, and that soon all stir ceased in his direction and I was left to enjoy my triumph and to listen with anxious interest to the strange and unintelligible sounds which accompanied the descent of the horseman down the face of the cliff, and finally to watch with a fascination, which drew me to my knees, the passage of that sparkling star of light hanging from his saddle. It crept to and fro across the side of the opposite mountain as he threaded its endless zigzags and finally disappeared over the brow into the invisible canyons beyond.

With the disappearance of this beacon came lassitude and sleep, through whose hazy atmosphere floated wild sentences from the sick tent, which showed that the patient was back again in Nevada, quarreling over the price of a horse which was to carry him beyond the reach of some threatening avalanche.

When next morning I came to depart, the doctor took me by both hands and looked me straight in the eyes.

"You heard," he said.

"How do you know?" I asked.

"I can tell a satisfied man when I see him," he growled, throwing down my hands with that same humorous twinkle in his eyes which had encouraged me from the first.

I made no answer, but I shall remember the lesson.

One detail more. When I stared on my own descent I found why the leggings, with which I had been provided, were so indispensable. I was not allowed to ride; indeed, riding down those steep declivities was impossible. No horse could preserve his balance with a rider on his back. I slid, so did my horse, and only in the valley beneath did we come together again.

VIII. ARREST

The success of this interview provoked other attempts on the part of the reporters who now flocked into the Southwest. Ere long particulars began to pour in of Mr. Fairbrother's painful journey south, after his illness set in. The clerk of the hotel in El Moro, where the great mine-owner's name was found registered at the time of the murder, told a story which made very good reading for those who were more interested in the sufferings and experiences of the millionaire husband of the murdered lady than in those of the unhappy but comparatively insignificant man upon whom public opinion had cast the odium of her death.

It seems that when the first news came of the great crime which had taken place in New York, Mr. Fairbrother was absent from the hotel on a prospecting tour through the adjacent mountains. Couriers had been sent after him, and it was one of these who finally brought him into town. He had been found wandering alone on horseback among the defiles of an untraveled region, sick and almost incoherent from fever. Indeed, his condition was such that neither the courier nor such others as saw him had the heart to tell him the dreadful news from New York, or even to show him the papers. To their great relief, he betrayed no curiosity in them. All he wanted was a berth in the first train going south, and this was an easy way for them out of a great responsibility. They listened to his wishes and saw him safely aboard, with such alacrity and with so many precautions against his being disturbed that they have never doubted that he left El Moro in total ignorance, not only of the circumstances of his great bereavement, but of the bereavement itself.

This ignorance, which he appeared to have carried with him to the Placide, was regarded by those who knew him best as proving the truth of the affirmation elicited from him in the pauses of his delirium of the genuineness of the stone which had passed from his hands to those of his wife at the time of their separation; and, further despatches coming in, some private and some official, but all insisting upon the fact that it would be weeks before he would be in a condition to submit to any sort of examination on a subject so painful, the authorities in New York decided to wait no longer for his testimony, but to proceed at once with the inquest.

Great as is the temptation to give a detailed account of proceedings which were of such moment to myself, and to every word of which I listened with the eagerness of a novice and the anguish of a woman who sees her lover's reputation at the mercy of a verdict which may stigmatize him as a possible criminal, I see no reason for encumbering my narrative with what, for the most part, would be a mere repetition of facts already known to you.

Mr. Durand's intimate and suggestive connection with this crime, the explanations he had to give of this connection, frequently bizarre and, I must acknowledge, not always convincing,—nothing could alter these nor change the fact of the undoubted cowardice he displayed in hiding Mrs. Fairbrother's gloves in my unfortunate little bag.

As for the mystery of the warning, it remained as much of a mystery as ever. Nor did any better success follow an attempt to fix the ownership of the stiletto, though a half-day was exhausted in an endeavor to show that the latter might have come into Mr. Durand's possession in some of the many visits he was shown to have made of late to various curio-shops in and out of New York City.[1]

I had expected all this, just as I had expected Mr. Grey to be absent from the proceedings and his testimony ignored. But this expectation did not make the ordeal any easier, and when I noticed the effect of witness after witness leaving the stand without having improved Mr. Durand's position by a jot or offering any new clue capable of turning suspicion into other directions, I felt my spirit harden and my purpose strengthen till I hardly knew myself. I must have frightened my uncle, for his hand was always on my arm and his chiding voice in my ear, bidding me beware, not only for my own sake and his, but for that of Mr. Durand, whose eye was seldom away from my face.

The verdict, however, was not the one I had so deeply dreaded. While it did not exonerate Mr. Durand, it did not openly accuse him, and I was on the point of giving him a smile of congratulation and renewed hope when I saw my little detective—the one who had spied the gloves in my bag at the ball—advance and place his hand upon his arm.

The police had gone a step further than the coroner's jury, and Mr. Durand was arrested, before my eyes, on a charge of murder.

---

[1] Mr. Durand's visits to the curio-shops, as explained by him, were made with a view of finding a casket in which to place his diamond. This explanation was looked upon with as much doubt as the others he had offered where the situation seemed to be of a compromising character.

IX. THE MOUSE NIBBLES AT THE NET

The next day saw me at police headquarters begging an interview from the inspector, with the intention of confiding to him a theory which must either cost me his sympathy or open the way to a new inquiry, which I felt sure would lead to Mr. Durand's complete exoneration.

I chose this gentleman for my confidant, from among all those with whom I had been brought in contact by my position as witness in a case of this magnitude, first, because he had been present at the most tragic moment of my life, and secondly, because I was conscious of a sympathetic bond between us which would insure me a kind hearing. However ridiculous my idea might appear to him, I was assured that he would treat me with consideration and not visit whatever folly I might be guilty of on the head of him for whom I risked my reputation for good sense.

Nor was I disappointed in this. Inspector Dalzell's air was fatherly and his tone altogether gentle as, in reply to my excuses for troubling him with my opinions, he told me that in a case of such importance he was glad to receive the impressions even of such a prejudiced little partizan as myself. The word fired me, and I spoke.

"You consider Mr. Durand guilty, and so do many others, I fear, in spite of his long record for honesty and uprightness. And why? Because you will not admit the possibility of another person's guilt,—a person standing so high in private and public estimation that the very idea seems preposterous and little short of insulting to the country of which he is an acknowledged ornament."

"My dear!"

The inspector had actually risen. His expression and whole attitude showed shock. But I did not quail; I only subdued my manner and spoke with quieter conviction.

"I am aware," said I, "how words so daring must impress you. But listen, sir; listen to what I have to say before you utterly condemn me. I acknowledge that it is the frightful position into which I threw Mr. Durand by my officious attempt to right him which has driven me to make this second effort to fix the crime on the only other man who had possible access to Mrs. Fairbrother at the fatal moment. How could I live in inaction? How could you expect me to weigh for a moment this foreigner's reputation against that of my own lover? If I have reasons—"

"Reasons!"

"—reasons which would appeal to all; if instead of this person's having an international reputation at his back he had been a simple gentleman like Mr. Durand,—would you not consider me entitled to speak?"

"Certainly, but—"

"You have no confidence in my reasons, Inspector; they may not weigh against that splash of blood on Mr. Durand's shirt-front, but such as they are I must give them. But first, it will be necessary for you to accept for the nonce Mr. Durand's statements as true. Are you willing to do this?"

"I will try."

"Then, a harder thing yet,—to put some confidence in my judgment. I saw the man and did not like him long before any intimation of the evening's tragedy had turned suspicion on any one. I watched him as I watched others. I saw that he had not come to the ball to please Mr. Ramsdell or for any pleasure he himself hoped to reap from social intercourse, but for some purpose much more important, and that this purpose was connected with Mrs. Fairbrother's diamond. Indifferent, almost morose before she came upon the scene, he brightened to a surprising extent the moment he found himself in her presence. Not because she was a beautiful woman, for he scarcely honored her face or even her superb figure with a look. All his glances were centered on her large fan, which, in swaying to and fro, alternately hid and revealed the splendor on her breast; and when by chance it hung suspended for a moment in her forgetful hand and he caught a full glimpse of the great gem, I perceived such a change in his face that, if nothing more had occurred that night to give prominence to this woman and her diamond, I should have carried home the conviction that interests of no common import lay behind a feeling so extraordinarily displayed."

"Fanciful, my dear Miss Van Arsdale I Interesting, but fanciful."

"I know. I have not yet touched on fact. But facts are coming, Inspector."

He stared. Evidently he was not accustomed to hear the law laid down in this fashion by a midget of my proportions.

"Go on," said he; "happily, I have no clerk here to listen."

"I would not speak if you had. These are words for but one ear as yet. Not even my uncle suspects the direction of my thoughts."

"Proceed," he again enjoined.

Upon which I plunged into my subject.

"Mrs. Fairbrother wore the real diamond, and no imitation, to the ball. Of this I feel sure. The bit of glass or paste displayed to the coroner's jury was bright enough, but it was not the star of light I saw burning on her breast as she passed me on her way to the alcove."

"Miss Van Arsdale!"

"The interest which Mr. Durand displayed in it, the marked excitement into which he was thrown by his first view of its size and splendor, confirm in my mind the evidence which he gave on oath (and he is a well-known diamond expert, you know, and must have been very well aware that he would injure rather than help his cause by this admission) that at that time he believed the stone to be real and of immense value. Wearing such a gem, then, she entered the fatal alcove, and, with a smile on her face, prepared to employ her fascinations on whoever chanced to come within their reach. But now something happened. Please let me tell it my own way. A shout from the driveway, or a bit of snow thrown against the window, drew her attention to a man standing below, holding up a note fastened to the end of a whip-handle. I do not know whether or not you have found that man. If you have—" The inspector made no sign. "I judge that you have not, so I may go on with my suppositions. Mrs. Fairbrother took in this note. She may have expected it and for this reason chose the alcove to sit in, or it may have been a surprise to her. Probably we shall never know the whole truth about it; but what we can know and do, if you are still holding to our compact and viewing this crime in the light of Mr. Durand's explanations, is that it made a change in her and made her anxious to rid herself of the diamond. It has been decided that the hurried scrawl should read, 'Take warning. He means to be at the ball. Expect trouble if you do not give him the diamond,' or something to that effect. But why was it passed up to her unfinished? Was the haste too great? I hardly think so. I believe in another explanation, which points with startling directness to the possibility that the person referred to in this broken communication was not Mr. Durand, but one whom I need not name; and that the reason you have failed to find the messenger, of whose appearance you have received definite information, is that you have not looked among the servants of a certain distinguished visitor in town. Oh," I burst forth with feverish volubility, as I saw the inspector's lips open in what could not fail to be a sarcastic utterance, "I know what you feel tempted to reply. Why should a servant deliver a warning against his own master? If you will be patient with me you will soon see; but first I wish to make it clear that Mrs. Fairbrother, having received this warning just before Mr. Durand appeared in the alcove,—reckless, scheming woman that she was!— sought to rid herself of the object against which it was directed in the way we have temporarily accepted as true. Relying on her arts, and possibly misconceiving the nature of Mr. Durand's interest in her, she hands over the diamond hidden in her rolled-up gloves, which he, without suspicion, carries away with him, thus linking himself indissolubly to a great crime of which another was the perpetrator. That other, or so I believe from my very heart of hearts, was the man I saw leaning against the wall at the foot of the alcove a few minutes before I passed into the supper-room."

I stopped with a gasp, hardly able to meet the stern and forbidding look with which the inspector sought to restrain what he evidently considered the senseless ravings of a child. But I had come there to speak, and I hastily proceeded before the rebuke thus expressed could formulate itself into words.

"I have some excuse for a declaration so monstrous. Perhaps I am the only person who can satisfy you in regard to a certain fact about which you have expressed some curiosity. Inspector, have you ever solved the mystery of the two broken coffee-cups found amongst the debris at Mrs. Fairbrother's feet? It did not come out in the inquest, I noticed."

"Not yet," he cried, "but—you can not tell me anything about them!"

"Possibly not. But I can tell you this: When I reached the supper-room door that evening I looked back and, providentially or otherwise—only the future can determine that—detected Mr. Grey in the act of lifting two cups from a tray left by some waiter on a table standing just outside the reception-room door. I did not see where he carried them; I only saw his face turned toward the alcove; and as there was no other lady there, or anywhere near there, I have dared to think—"

Here the inspector found speech.

"You saw Mr. Grey lift two cups and turn toward the alcove at a moment we all know to have been critical? You should have told me this before. He may be a possible witness."

I scarcely listened. I was too full of my own argument.

"There were other people in the hall, especially at my end of it. A perfect throng was coming from the billiard-room, where the dancing had been, and it might easily be that he could both enter and leave that secluded spot without attracting attention. He had shown too early and much too unmistakably his lack of interest in the general company for his every movement to be watched as at his first arrival. But this is simple conjecture; what I have to say next is evidence. The stiletto—have you studied it, sir? I have, from the pictures. It is very quaint; and among the devices on the handle is one that especially attracted my attention. See! This is what I mean." And I handed him a drawing which I had made with some care in expectation of this very interview.

He surveyed it with some astonishment.

"I understand," I pursued in trembling tones, for I was much affected by my own daring, "that no one has so far succeeded in tracing this weapon to its owner. Why didn't your experts study heraldry and the devices of great houses? They would have found that this one is not unknown in England. I can tell you on whose blazon it can often be seen, and so could—Mr. Grey."

X. I ASTONISH THE INSPECTOR

I was not the only one to tremble now. This man of infinite experience and daily contact with crime had turned as pale as ever I myself had done in face of a threatening calamity.

"I shall see about this," he muttered, crumpling the paper in his hand. "But this is a very terrible business you are plunging me into. I sincerely hope that you are not heedlessly misleading me."

"I am correct in my facts, if that is what you mean," said I. "The stiletto is an English heirloom, and bears on its blade, among other devices, that of Mr. Grey's family on the female side. But that is not all I want to say. If the blow was struck to obtain the diamond, the shock of not finding it on his victim must have been terrible. Now Mr. Grey's heart, if my whole theory is not utterly false, was set upon obtaining this stone. Your eye was not on him as mine was when you made your appearance in the hall with the recovered jewel. He showed astonishment, eagerness, and a determination which finally led him forward, as you know, with the request to take the diamond in his hand. Why did he want to take it in his hand? And why, having taken it, did he drop it—a diamond supposed to be worth an ordinary man's fortune? Because he was startled by a cry he chose to consider the traditional one of his family proclaiming death? Is it likely, sir? Is it conceivable even that any such cry as we heard could, in this day and generation, ring through such an assemblage, unless it came with ventriloquial power from his own lips? You observed that he turned his back; that his face was hidden from us. Discreet and reticent as we have all been, and careful in our criticisms of so bizarre an event, there still must be many to question the reality of such superstitious fears, and some to ask if such a sound could be without human agency, and a very guilty agency, too. Inspector, I am but a child in your estimation, and I feel my position in this matter much more keenly than you do, but I would not be true to the man whom I have unwittingly helped to place in his present unenviable position if I did not tell you that, in my judgment, this cry was a spurious one, employed by the gentleman himself as an excuse for dropping the stone."

"And why should he wish to drop the stone?"

"Because of the fraud he meditated. Because it offered him an opportunity for substituting a false stone for the real. Did you not notice a change in the aspect of this jewel dating from this very moment? Did it shine with as much brilliancy in your hand when you received it back as when you passed it over?"

"Nonsense! I do not know; it is all too absurd for argument." Yet he did stop to argue, saying in the next breath: "You forget that the stone has a setting. Would you claim that this gentleman of family, place and political distinction had planned this hideous crime with sufficient premeditation to have provided himself with the exact counterpart of a brooch which it is highly improbable he ever saw? You would make him out a Cagliostro or something worse. Miss Van Arsdale, I fear your theory will topple over of its own weight."

He was very patient with me; he did not show me the door.

"Yet such a substitution took place, and took place that evening," I insisted. "The bit of paste shown us at the inquest was never the gem Mrs. Fairbrother wore on entering the alcove. Besides, where all is sensation, why cavil at one more improbability? Mr. Grey may have come over to America for no other reason. He is known as a collector, and when a man has a passion for diamond-getting—"

"He is known as a collector?"

"In his own country."

"I was not told that."

"Nor I. But I found it out."

"How, my dear child, how?"

"By a cablegram or so."

"You—cabled—his name—to England?"

"No, Inspector; uncle has a code, and I made use of it to ask a friend in London for a list of the most noted diamond fanciers in the country. Mr. Grey's name was third on the list."

He gave me a look in which admiration was strangely blended with doubt and apprehension.

"You are making a brave struggle," said he, "but it is a hopeless one."

"I have one more confidence to repose in you. The nurse who has charge of Miss Grey was in my class in the hospital. We love each other, and to her I dared appeal on one point. Inspector—" here my voice unconsciously fell as he impetuously drew nearer—"a note was sent from that sick chamber on the night of the ball,—a note surreptitiously written by Miss Grey, while the nurse was in an adjoining room. The messenger was Mr. Grey's valet, and its destination the house in which her father was enjoying his position as chief guest. She says that it was meant for him, but I have dared to think that the valet would tell a different story. My friend did not see what her patient wrote, but she acknowledged that if her patient wrote more than two words the result must have been an unintelligible scrawl, since she was too weak to hold a pencil firmly, and so nearly blind that she would have had to feel her way over the paper."

The inspector started, and, rising hastily, went to his desk, from which he presently brought the scrap of paper which had already figured in the inquest as the mysterious communication taken from Mrs. Fairbrother's hand by the coroner. Pressing it out flat, he took another look at it, then glanced up in visible discomposure.

"It has always looked to us as if written in the dark, by an agitated hand; but—"

I said nothing; the broken and unfinished scrawl was sufficiently eloquent.

"Did your friend declare Miss Grey to have written with a pencil and on a small piece of unruled paper?"

"Yes, the pencil was at her bedside; the paper was torn from a book which lay there. She did not put the note when written in an envelope, but gave it to the valet just as it was. He is an old man and had come to her room for some final orders."

"The nurse saw all this? Has she that book?"

"No, it went out next morning, with the scraps. It was some pamphlet, I believe."

The inspector turned the morsel of paper over and over in his hand.

"What is this nurse's name?"

"Henrietta Pierson."

"Does she share your doubts?"

"I can not say."

"You have seen her often?"

"No, only the one time."

"Is she discreet?"

"Very. On this subject she will be like the grave unless forced by you to speak."

"And Miss Grey?"

"She is still ill, too ill to be disturbed by questions, especially on so delicate a topic. But she is getting well fast. Her father's fears as we heard them expressed on one memorable occasion were ill founded, sir."

Slowly the inspector inserted this scrap of paper between the folds of his pocketbook. He did not give me another look, though I stood trembling before him. Was he in any way convinced or was he simply seeking for the most considerate way in which to dismiss me and my abominable theory? I could not gather his intentions from his expression, and was feeling very faint and heart-sick when he suddenly turned upon me with the remark:

"A girl as ill as you say Miss Grey was must have had some very pressing matter on her mind to attempt to write and send a message under such difficulties. According to your idea, she had some notion of her father's designs and wished to warn Mrs. Fairbrother against them. But don't you see that such conduct as this would be preposterous, nay, unparalleled in persons of their distinction? You must find some other explanation for Miss Grey's seemingly mysterious action, and I an agent of crime other than one of England's most reputable statesmen."

"So that Mr. Durand is shown the same consideration, I am content," said I. "It is the truth and the truth only I desire. I am willing to trust my cause with you."

He looked none too grateful for this confidence. Indeed, now that I look back on this scene, I do not wonder that he shrank from the responsibility thus foisted upon him.

"What do you want me to do?" he asked.

"Prove something. Prove that I am altogether wrong or altogether right. Or if proof is not possible, pray allow me the privilege of doing what I can myself to clear up the matter."

"You?"

There was apprehension, disapprobation, almost menace in his tone. I bore it with as steady and modest a glance as possible, saying, when I thought he was about to speak again:

"I will do nothing without your sanction. I realize the dangers of this inquiry and the disgrace that would follow if our attempt was suspected before proof reached a point sufficient to justify it. It is not an open attack I meditate, but one—"

Here I whispered in his ear for several minutes, when I had finished he gave me a prolonged stare, then he laid his hand on my head.

"You are a little wonder," he declared. "But your ideas are very quixotic, very. However," he added, suddenly growing grave, "something, I must admit, may be excused a young girl who finds herself forced to choose between the guilt of her lover and that of a man esteemed great by the world, but altogether removed from her and her natural sympathies."

"You acknowledge, then, that it lies between these two?"

"I see no third," said he.

I drew a breath of relief.

"Don't deceive yourself, Miss Van Arsdale; it is not among the possibilities that Mr. Grey has had any connection with this crime. He is an eccentric man, that's all."

"But—but—"

"I shall do my duty. I shall satisfy you and myself on certain points, and if—" I hardly breathed "—there is the least doubt, I will see you again and—"

The change he saw in me frightened away the end of his sentence. Turning upon me with some severity, he declared: "There are nine hundred and ninety-nine chances in a thousand that my next word to you will be to prepare yourself for Mr. Durand's arraignment and trial. But an infinitesimal chance remains to the contrary. If you choose to trust to it, I can only admire your pluck and the great confidence you show in your unfortunate lover."

And with this half-hearted encouragement I was forced to be content, not only for that day, but for many days, when—

XI. THE INSPECTOR ASTONISHES ME

But before I proceed to relate what happened at the end of those two weeks, I must say a word or two in regard to what happened during them.

Nothing happened to improve Mr. Durand's position, and nothing openly to compromise Mr. Grey's. Mr. Fairbrother, from whose testimony many of us hoped something would yet be gleaned calculated to give a turn to the suspicion now centered on one man, continued ill in New Mexico; and all that could be learned from him of any importance was contained in a short letter dictated from his bed, in which he affirmed that the diamond, when it left him, was in a unique setting procured by himself in France; that he knew of no other jewel similarly mounted, and that if the false gem was set according to his own description, the probabilities were that the imitation stone had been put in place of the real one under his wife's direction and in some workshop in New York, as she was not the woman to take the trouble to send abroad for anything she could get done in this country. The description followed. It coincided with the one we all knew.

This was something of a blow to me. Public opinion would naturally reflect that of the husband, and it would require very strong evidence indeed to combat a logical supposition of this kind with one so forced and seemingly extravagant as that upon which my own theory was based. Yet truth often transcends imagination, and, having confidence in the inspector's integrity, I subdued my impatience for a week, almost for two, when my suspense and rapidly culminating dread of some action being taken against Mr. Durand were suddenly cut short by a message from the inspector, followed by his speedy presence in my uncle's house.

We have a little room on our parlor floor, very snug and secluded, and in this room I received him. Seldom have I dreaded a meeting more and seldom have I been met with greater kindness and consideration. He was so kind that I feared he had only disappointing news to communicate, but his first words reassured me. He said:

"I have come to you on a matter of importance. We have found enough truth in the suppositions you advanced at our last interview to warrant us in the attempt you yourself proposed for the elucidation of this mystery. That this is the most risky and altogether the most unpleasant duty which I have encountered during my several years of service, I am willing to acknowledge to one so sensible and at the same time of so much modesty as yourself. This English gentleman has a reputation which lifts him far above any unworthy suspicion, and were it not for the favorable impression made upon us by Mr. Durand in a long talk we had with him last night, I would sooner resign my place than pursue this matter against him. Success would create a horror on both sides the water unprecedented during my career, while failure would bring down ridicule on us which would destroy the prestige of the whole force. Do you see my difficulty, Miss Van Arsdale? We can not even approach this haughty and highly reputable Englishman with questions without calling down on us the wrath of the whole English nation. We must be sure before we make a move, and for us to be sure where the evidence is all circumstantial, I know of no better plan than the one you were pleased to suggest, which, at the time, I was pleased to call quixotic."

Drawing a long breath I surveyed him timidly. Never had I so realized my presumption or experienced such a thrill of joy in my frightened yet elated heart. They believed in Anson's innocence and they trusted me. Insignificant as I was, it was to my exertions this great result was due. As I realized this, I felt my heart swell and my throat close. In despair of speaking I held out my hands. He took them kindly and seemed to be quite satisfied.

"Such a little, trembling, tear-filled Amazon!" he cried. "Shall you have courage to undertake the task before you? If not—"

"Oh, but I have," said I. "It is your goodness and the surprise of it all which unnerves me. I can go through what we have planned if you think the secret of my personality and interest in Mr. Durand can be kept from the people I go among."

"It can if you will follow our advice implicitly. You say that you know the doctor and that he stands ready to recommend you in case Miss Pierson withdraws her services."

"Yes, he is eager to give me a chance. He was a college mate of my father's."

"How will you explain to him your wish to enter upon your duties under another name?"

"Very simply. I have already told him that the publicity given my name in the late proceedings has made me very uncomfortable; that my first case of nursing would require all my self-possession and that if he did not think it wrong I should like to go to it under my mother's name. He made no dissent and I think I can persuade him that I would do much better work as Miss Ayers than as the too well-known Miss Van Arsdale."

"You have great powers of persuasion. But may you not meet people at the hotel who know you?"

"I shall try to avoid people; and, if my identity is discovered, its effect or non-effect upon one we find it difficult to mention will give us our clue. If he has no guilty interest in the crime, my connection with it as a witness will not disturb him. Besides, two days of unsuspicious acceptance of me as Miss Grey's nurse are all I want. I shall take immediate opportunity, I assure you, to make the test I mentioned. But how much confidence you will have to repose in me! I comprehend all the importance of my undertaking, and shall work as if my honor, as well as yours, were at stake."

"I am sure you will." Then for the first time in my life I was glad that I was small and plain rather than tall and fascinating like so many of my friends, for he said: "If you had been a triumphant beauty, depending on your charms as a woman to win people to your will, we should never have listened to your proposition or risked our reputation in your hands. It is your wit, your earnestness and your quiet determination which have impressed us. You see I speak plainly. I do so because I respect you. And now to business."

Details followed. After these were well understood between us, I ventured to say: "Do you object—would it be asking too much—if I requested some enlightenment as to what facts you have discovered about Mr. Grey which go to substantiate my theory? I might work more intelligently."

"No, Miss Van Arsdale, you would not work more intelligently, and you know it. But you have the natural curiosity of one whose very heart is bound up in this business. I could deny you what you ask but I won't, for I want you to work with quiet confidence, which you would not do if your mind were taken up with doubts and questions. Miss Van Arsdale, one surmise of yours was correct. A man was sent that night to the Ramsdell house with a note from Miss Grey. We know this because he boasted of it to one of the bell-boys before he went out, saying that he was going to have a glimpse of one of the swellest parties of the season. It is also true that this man was Mr. Grey's valet, an old servant who came over with him from England. But what adds weight to all this and makes us regard the whole affair with suspicion, is the additional fact that this man received his dismissal the following morning and has not been seen since by any one we could reach. This looks bad to begin with, like the suppression of evidence, you know. Then Mr. Grey has not been the same man since that night. He is full of care and this care is not entirely in connection with his daughter, who is doing very well and bids fair to be up in a few days. But all this would be nothing if we had not received advices from England which prove that Mr. Grey's visit here has an element of mystery in it. There was every reason for his remaining in his own country, where a political crisis is approaching, yet he crossed the water, bringing his sickly daughter with him. The explanation as volunteered by one who knew him well was this: That only his desire to see or acquire some precious object for his collection could have taken him across the ocean at this time, nothing else rivaling his interest in governmental affairs. Still this would be nothing if a stiletto similar to the one employed in this crime had not once formed part of a collection of curios belonging to a cousin of his whom he often visited. This stiletto has been missing for some time, stolen, as the owner declared, by some unknown person. All this looks bad enough, but when I tell you that a week before the fatal ball at Mr. Ramsdell's, Mr. Grey made a tour of the jewelers on Broadway and, with the pretext of buying a diamond for his daughter, entered into a talk about famous stones, ending always with some question about the Fairbrother gem, you will see that his interest in that stone is established and that it only remains for us to discover if that interest is a guilty one. I can not believe this possible, but you have our leave to make your experiment and see. Only do not count too much on his superstition. If he is the deep-dyed criminal you imagine, the cry which startled us all at a certain critical instant was raised by himself and for the purpose you suggested. None of the sensitiveness often shown by a man who has been surprised into crime will be his. Relying on his reputation and the prestige of his great name, he will, if he thinks himself under fire, face every shock unmoved."

"I see; I understand. He must believe himself all alone; then, the natural man may appear. I thank you, Inspector. That idea is of inestimable value to me, and

I shall act on it. I do not say immediately; not on the first day, and possibly not on the second, but as soon as opportunity offers for my doing what I have planned with any chance of success. And now, advise me how to circumvent my uncle and aunt, who must never know to what an undertaking I have committed myself."

Inspector Dalzell spared me another fifteen minutes, and this last detail was arranged. Then he rose to go. As he turned from me he said:

"To-morrow?"

And I answered with a full heart, but a voice clear as my purpose:

"To-morrow."

XII. ALMOST

"This is your patient. Your new nurse, my dear. What did you say your name is? Miss Ayers?"

"Yes, Mr. Grey, Alice Ayers."

"Oh, what a sweet name!"

This expressive greeting, from the patient herself, was the first heart-sting I received,—a sting which brought a flush into my cheek which I would fain have kept down.

"Since a change of nurses was necessary, I am glad they sent me one like you," the feeble, but musical voice went on, and I saw a wasted but eager hand stretched out.

In a whirl of strong feeling I advanced to take it. I had not counted on such a reception. I had not expected any bond of congeniality to spring up between this high-feeling English girl and myself to make my purpose hateful to me. Yet, as I stood there looking down at her bright if wasted face, I felt that it would be very easy to love so gentle and cordial a being, and dreaded raising my eyes to the gentleman at my side lest I should see something in him to hamper me, and make this attempt, which I had undertaken in such loyalty of spirit, a misery to myself and ineffectual to the man I had hoped to save by it. When I did look up and catch the first beams of Mr. Grey's keen blue eyes fixed inquiringly on me, I neither knew what to think nor how to act. He was tall and firmly knit, and had an intellectual aspect altogether. I was conscious of regarding him with a decided feeling of awe, and found myself forgetting why I had come there, and what my suspicions were,—suspicions which had carried hope with them, hope for myself and hope for my lover, who would never escape the opprobrium, even if he did the punishment, of this great crime, were this, the only other person who could possibly be associated with it, found to be the fine, clear-souled man he appeared to be in this my first interview with him.

Perceiving very soon that his apprehensions in my regard were limited to a fear lest I should not feel at ease in my new home under the restraint of a presence more accustomed to intimidate than attract strangers, I threw aside all doubts of myself and met the advances of both father and daughter with that quiet confidence which my position there demanded.

The result both gratified and grieved me. As a nurse entering on her first case I was happy; as a woman with an ulterior object in view verging on the audacious and unspeakable, I was wretched and regretful and just a little shaken in the conviction which had hitherto upheld me.

I was therefore but poorly prepared to meet the ordeal which awaited me, when, a little later in the day, Mr. Grey called me into the adjoining room, and, after saying that it would afford him great relief to go out for an hour or so, asked if I were afraid to be left alone with my patient.

"O no, sir—" I began, but stopped in secret dismay. I was afraid, but not on account of her condition; rather on account of my own. What if I should be led into betraying my feelings on finding myself under no other eye than her own!

What if the temptation to probe her poor sick mind should prove stronger than my duty toward her as a nurse!

My tones were hesitating but Mr. Grey paid little heed; his mind was too fixed on what he wished to say himself.

"Before I go," said he, "I have a request to make—I may as well say a caution to give you. Do not, I pray, either now or at any future time, carry or allow any one else to carry newspapers into Miss Grey's room. They are just now too alarming. There has been, as you know, a dreadful murder in this city. If she caught one glimpse of the headlines, or saw so much as the name of Fairbrother—which—which is a name she knows, the result might be very hurtful to her. She is not only extremely sensitive from illness but from temperament. Will you be careful?"

"I shall be careful."

It was such an effort for me to say these words, to say anything in the state of mind into which I had been thrown by his unexpected allusion to this subject, that I unfortunately drew his attention to myself and it was with what I felt to be a glance of doubt that he added with decided emphasis:

"You must consider this whole subject as a forbidden one in this family. Only cheerful topics are suitable for the sick-room. If Miss Grey attempts to introduce any other, stop her. Do not let her talk about anything which will not be conducive to her speedy recovery. These are the only instructions I have to give you; all others must come from her physician."

I made some reply with as little show of emotion as possible. It seemed to satisfy him, for his face cleared as he kindly observed:

"You have a very trustworthy look for one so young. I shall rest easy while you are with her, and I shall expect you to be always with her when I am not. Every moment, mind. She is never to be left alone with gossiping servants. If a word is mentioned in her hearing about this crime which seems to be in everybody's mouth, I shall feel forced, greatly as I should regret the fad, to blame you."

This was a heart-stroke, but I kept up bravely, changing color perhaps, but not to such a marked degree as to arouse any deeper suspicion in his mind than that I had been wounded in my amour propre.

"She shall be well guarded," said I. "You may trust me to keep from her all avoidable knowledge of this crime."

He bowed and I was about to leave his presence, when he detained me by remarking with the air of one who felt that some explanation was necessary:

"I was at the ball where this crime took place. Naturally it has made a deep impression on me and would on her if she heard of it."

"Assuredly," I murmured, wondering if he would say more and how I should have the courage to stand there and listen if he did.

"It is the first time I have ever come in contact with crime," he went on with what, in one of his reserved nature, seemed a hardly natural insistence. "I could well have been spared the experience. A tragedy with which one has been even thus remotely connected produces a lasting effect upon the mind."

"Oh yes, oh yes!" I murmured, edging involuntarily toward the door. Did I not know? Had I not been there, too; I, little I, whom he stood gazing down upon from such a height, little realizing the fatality which united us and, what was even a more overwhelming thought to me at the moment, the fact that of all persons in the world the shrinking little being, into whose eyes he was then looking, was, perhaps, his greatest enemy and the one person, great or small, from whom he had the most to fear.

But I was no enemy to his gentle daughter and the relief I felt at finding myself thus cut off by my own promise from even the remotest communication with her on this forbidden subject was genuine and sincere.

But the father! What was I to think of the father? Alas! I could have but one thought, admirable as he appeared in all lights save the one in which his too evident connection with this crime had placed him. I spent the hours of the afternoon in alternately watching the sleeping face of my patient, too sweetly calm in its repose, or so it seemed, for the mind beneath to harbor such doubts as were shown in the warning I had ascribed to her, and vain efforts to explain by any other hypothesis than that of guilt, the extraordinary evidence which linked this man of great affairs and the loftiest repute to a crime involving both theft and murder.

Nor did the struggle end that night. It was renewed with still greater positiveness the next day, as I witnessed the glances which from time to time passed between this father and daughter,—glances full of doubt and question on both sides, but not exactly such doubt or such question as my suspicions called for. Or so I thought, and spent another day or two hesitating very much over my duty, when, coming unexpectedly upon Mr. Grey one evening, I felt all my doubts revive in view of the extraordinary expression of dread—I might with still greater truth say fear—which informed his features and made them, to my unaccustomed eyes, almost unrecognizable.

He was sitting at his desk in reverie over some papers which he seemed not to have touched for hours, and when, at some movement I made, he started up and met my eye, I could swear that his cheek was pale, the firm carriage of his body shaken, and the whole man a victim to some strong and secret apprehension he vainly sought to hide, when I ventured to tell him what I wanted, he made an effort and pulled himself together, but I had seen him with his mask off, and his usually calm visage and self-possessed mien could not again deceive me.

My duties kept me mainly at Miss Grey's bedside, but I had been provided with a little room across the hall, and to this room I retired very soon after this, for rest and a necessary understanding with myself.

For, in spite of this experience and my now settled convictions, my purpose required whetting. The indescribable charm, the extreme refinement and nobility of manner observable in both Mr. Grey and his daughter were producing their effect. I felt guilty; constrained. whatever my convictions, the impetus to act was leaving me. How could I recover it? By thinking of Anson Durand and his present disgraceful position.

Anson Durand! Oh, how the feeling surged up in my breast as that name slipped from my lips on crossing the threshold of my little room! Anson Durand, whom I believed innocent, whom I loved, but whom I was betraying with every moment of hesitation in which I allowed myself to indulge! what if the Honorable Mr. Grey is an eminent statesman, a dignified, scholarly, and to all appearance, high-minded man? what if my patient is sweet, dove-eyed and affectionate? Had not Anson qualities as excellent in their way, rights as certain, and a hold upon myself superior to any claims which another might advance? Drawing a much-crumpled little note from my pocket, I eagerly read it. It was the only one I had of his writing, the only letter he had ever written me. I had already re-read it a hundred times, but as I once more repeated to myself its well-known lines, I felt my heart grow strong and fixed in the determination which had brought me into this family.

Restoring the letter to its place, I opened my gripsack and from its inmost recesses drew forth an object which I had no sooner in hand than a natural sense of disquietude led me to glance apprehensively, first at the door, then at the window, though I had locked the one and shaded the other. It seemed as if some other eye besides my own must be gazing at what I held so gingerly in hand; that the walls were watching me, if nothing else, and the sensation this produced was so exactly like that of guilt (or what I imagined to be guilt), that I was forced to repeat once more to myself that it was not a good man's overthrow I sought, or even a bad man's immunity from punishment, but the truth, the absolute truth. No shame could equal that which I should feel if, by any over-delicacy now, I failed to save the man who trusted me.

The article which I held—have you guessed it?—was the stiletto with which Mrs. Fairbrother had been killed. It had been intrusted to me by the police for a definite purpose. The time for testing that purpose had come, or so nearly come, that I felt I must be thinking about the necessary ways and means.

Unwinding the folds of tissue paper in which the stiletto was wrapped, I scrutinized the weapon very carefully. Hitherto, I had seen only pictures of it, now, I had the article itself in my hand. It was not a natural one for a young woman to hold, a woman whose taste ran more toward healing than inflicting wounds, but I forced myself to forget why the end of its blade was rusty, and looked mainly at the devices which ornamented the handle. I had not been mistaken in them. They belonged to the house of Grey, and to none other. It was a legitimate inquiry I had undertaken. However the matter ended, I should always have these historic devices for my excuse.

My plan was to lay this dagger on Mr. Grey's desk at a moment when he would be sure to see it and I to see him. If he betrayed a guilty knowledge of this fatal steel; if, unconscious of my presence, he showed surprise and apprehension,—then we should know how to proceed; justice would be loosed from constraint and the police feel at liberty to approach him. It was a delicate task, this. I realized how delicate, when I had thrust the stiletto out of sight under my nurse's apron and started to cross the hall. Should I find the library clear? Would the opportunity be given me to approach his desk, or should I have to carry this guilty witness of a world-famous crime on into Miss Grey's room, and with its unholy outline pressing a semblance of itself upon my breast, sit at that innocent pillow, meet those innocent eyes, and answer the gentle inquiries which now and then fell from the sweetest lips I have ever seen smile into the face of a lonely, preoccupied stranger?

The arrangement of the rooms was such as made it necessary for me to pass through this sitting-room in order to reach my patient's bedroom.

With careful tread, so timed as not to appear stealthy, I accordingly advanced and pushed open the door. The room was empty. Mr. Grey was still with his daughter and I could cross the floor without fear. But never had I entered upon a task requiring more courage or one more obnoxious to my natural instincts. I hated each step I took, but I loved the man for whom I took those steps, and moved resolutely on. Only, as I reached the chair in which Mr. Grey was accustomed to sit, I found that it was easier to plan an action than to carry it out. Home life and the domestic virtues had always appealed to me more than a man's greatness. The position which this man held in his own country, his usefulness there, even his prestige as statesman and scholar, were facts, but very dreamy facts, to me, while his feelings as a father, the place he held in his daughter's heart—these were real to me, these I could understand; and it was of these and not of his place as a man, that this his favorite seat spoke to me. How often had I beheld him sit by the hour with his eye on the door behind which his one darling lay ill! Even now, it was easy for me to recall his face as I had sometimes caught a glimpse of it through the crack of the suddenly opened door, and I felt my breast heave and my hand falter as I drew forth the stiletto and moved to place it where his eye would fall upon it on his leaving his daughter's bedside.

But my hand returned quickly to my breast and fell hack again empty. A pile of letters lay before me on the open lid of the desk. The top one was addressed to me with the word "Important" written in the corner. I did not know the writing, but I felt that I should open and read this letter before committing myself or those who stood back of me to this desperate undertaking.

Glancing behind me and seeing that the door into Miss Grey's room was ajar, I caught up this letter and rushed with it back into my own room. As I surmised, it was from the inspector, and as I read it I realized that I had received it not one moment too soon. In language purposely non-committal, but of a meaning not to be mistaken, it advised me that some unforeseen facts had come to light which altered all former suspicions and made the little surprise I had planned no longer necessary.

There was no allusion to Mr. Durand but the final sentence ran:

"Drop all care and give your undivided attention to your patient."

XIII. THE MISSING RECOMMENDATION

My patient slept that night, but I did not. The shock given by this sudden cry of Halt! at the very moment I was about to make my great move, the uncertainty as to what it meant and my doubt of its effect upon Mr. Durand's position, put me on the anxious seat and kept my thoughts fully occupied till morning.

I was very tired and must have shown it, when, with the first rays of a very meager sun, Miss Grey softly unclosed her eyes and found me looking at her, for her smile had a sweet compassion in it, and she said as she pressed my hand:

"You must have watched me all night. I never saw any one look so tired,— or so good," she softly finished.

I had rather she had not uttered that last phrase. It did not fit me at the moment,—did not fit me, perhaps, at any time. Good! I! when my thoughts had not been with her, but with Mr. Durand; when the dominating feeling in my breast was not that of relief, but a vague regret that I had not been allowed to make my great test and so establish, to my own satisfaction, at least, the perfect innocence of my lover even at the cost of untold anguish to this confiding girl upon whose gentle spirit the very thought of crime would cast a deadly blight.

I must have flushed; certainly I showed some embarrassment, for her eyes brightened with shy laughter as she whispered:

"You do not like to be praised,—another of your virtues. You have too many. I have only one—I love my friends."

She did. One could see that love was life to her.

For an instant I trembled. How near I had been to wrecking this gentle soul! Was she safe yet? I was not sure. My own doubts were not satisfied. I awaited the papers with feverish impatience. They should contain news. News of what? Ah, that was the question!

"You will let me see my mail this morning, will you not?" she asked, as I busied myself about her.

"That is for the doctor to say," I smiled. "You are certainly better this morning."

"It is so hard for me not to be able to read his letters, or to write a word to relieve his anxiety."

Thus she told me her heart's secret, and unconsciously added another burden to my already too heavy load.

I was on my way to give some orders about my patient's breakfast, when Mr. Grey came into the sitting-room and met me face to face. He had a newspaper in his hand and my heart stood still as I noted his altered looks and disturbed manner. Were these due to anything he had found in those columns? It was with difficulty that I kept my eyes from the paper which he held in such a manner as to disclose its glaring head-lines. These I dared not read with his eyes fixed on mine.

"How is Miss Grey? How is my daughter?" he asked in great haste and uneasiness. "Is she better this morning, or—worse?"

"Better," I assured him, and was greatly astonished to see his brow instantly clear.

"Really?" he asked. "You really consider her better? The doctors say so' but I have not very much faith in doctors in a case like this," he added.

"I have seen no reason to distrust them," I protested. "Miss Grey's illness, while severe, does not appear to be of an alarming nature. But then I have had very little experience out of the hospital. I am young yet, Mr. Grey."

He looked as if he quite agreed with me in this estimate of myself, and, with a brow still clouded, passed into his daughter's room, the paper in his hand. Before I joined them I found and scanned another journal. Expecting great things, I was both surprised and disappointed to find only a small paragraph devoted to the Fairbrother case. In this it was stated that the authorities hoped for new light on this mystery as soon as they had located a certain witness, whose connection with the crime they had just discovered. No more, no less than was contained in Inspector Dalzell's letter. How could I bear it,—the suspense, the doubt,—and do my duty to my patient! Happily, I had no choice. I had been adjudged equal to this business and I must prove myself to be so. Perhaps my courage would revive after I had had my breakfast; perhaps then I should be able to fix upon the identity of the new witness,—something which I found myself incapable of at this moment.

These thoughts were on my mind as I crossed the rooms on my way back to Miss Grey's bedside. By the time I reached her door I was outwardly calm, as her first words showed:

"Oh, the cheerful smile! It makes me feel better in spite of myself."

If she could have seen into my heart!

Mr. Grey, who was leaning over the foot of the bed, cast me a quick glance which was not without its suspicion. Had he detected me playing a part, or were such doubts as he displayed the product simply of his own uneasiness? I was not able to decide, and, with this unanswered question added to the number already troubling me, I was forced to face the day which, for aught I knew, might be the precursor of many others equally trying and unsatisfactory.

But help was near. Before noon I received a message from my uncle to the effect that if I could be spared he would be glad to see me at his home as near three o'clock as possible. What could he want of me? I could not guess, and it was with great inner perturbation that, having won Mr. Grey's permission, I responded to his summons.

I found my uncle awaiting me in a carriage before his own door, and I took my seat at his side without the least idea of his purpose. I supposed that he had planned this ride that he might talk to me unreservedly and without fear of interruption. But I soon saw that he had some very different object in view, for not only did he start down town instead of up, but his conversation, such as it was, confined itself to generalities and studiously avoided the one topic of supreme interest to us both.

At last, as we turned into Bleecker Street, I let my astonishment and perplexity appear.

"Where are we bound?" I asked. "It can not be that you are taking me to see Mr. Durand?"

"No," said he, and said no more.

"Ah, Police Headquarters!" I faltered as the carriage made another turn and drew up before a building I had reason to remember. "Uncle, what am I to do here?"

"See a friend," he answered, as he helped me to alight. Then as I followed him in some bewilderment, he whispered in my ear: "Inspector Dalzell. He wants a few minutes conversation with you."

Oh, the weight which fell from my shoulders at these words! I was to hear, then, what had intervened between me and my purpose. The wearing night I had anticipated was to be lightened with some small spark of knowledge. I had confidence enough in the kind-hearted inspector to be sure of that. I caught at my uncle's arm and squeezed it delightedly, quite oblivious of the curious glances I must have received from the various officials we passed on our way to the inspector's office.

We found him waiting for us, and I experienced such pleasure at sight of his kind and earnest face that I hardly noticed uncle's sly retreat till the door closed behind him.

"Oh, Inspector, what has happened?" I impetuously exclaimed in answer to his greeting. "Something that will help Mr. Durand without disturbing Mr. Grey—have you as good news for me as that?"

"Hardly," he answered, moving up a chair and seating me in it with a fatherly air which, under the circumstances, was more discouraging than consolatory. "We have simply heard of a new witness, or rather a fact has come to light which has turned our inquiries into a new direction."

"And—and—you can not tell me what this fact is?" I faltered as he showed no intention of adding anything to this very unsatisfactory explanation.

"I should not, but you were willing to do so much for us I must set aside my principles a little and do something for you. After all, it is only forestalling the reporters by a day. Miss Van Arsdale, this is the story: Yesterday morning a man was shown into this room, and said that he had information to give which might possibly prove to have some bearing on the Fairbrother case. I had seen the man before and recognized him at the first glance as one of the witnesses who made the inquest unnecessarily tedious. Do you remember Jones, the caterer, who had only two or three facts to give and yet who used up the whole afternoon in trying to state those facts?"

"I do, indeed," I answered.

"Well, he was the man, and I own that I was none too delighted to see him. But he was more at his ease with me than I expected, and I soon learned what he had to tell. It was this: One of his men had suddenly left him, one of his very best men, one of those who had been with him in the capacity of waiter at the Ramsdell ball. It was not uncommon for his men to leave him, but they usually gave notice. This man gave no notice; he simply did not show up at the usual hour. This was a week or two ago. Jones, having a liking for the man, who was an excellent waiter, sent a messenger to his lodging-house to see if he were ill. But he had left his lodgings with as little ceremony as he had left the caterer.

"This, under ordinary circumstances, would have ended the business, but there being some great function in prospect, Jones did not feel like losing so good a man without making an effort to recover him, so he looked up his references in the hope of obtaining some clue to his present whereabouts.

"He kept all such matters in a special book and expected to have no trouble in finding the man's name, James Wellgood, or that of his former employer But when he came to consult this book, he was astonished to find that nothing was recorded against this man's name but the date of his first employment—March 15.

"Had he hired him without a recommendation? He would not be likely to, yet the page was clear of all reference; only the name and the date. But the date! You have already noted its significance, and later he did, too. The day of the Ramsdell ball! The day of the great murder! As he recalled the incidents of that day he understood why the record of Wellgood's name was unaccompanied by the usual reference. It had been a difficult day all round. The function was an important one, and the weather bad. There was, besides, an unusual shortage in his number of assistants. Two men had that very morning been laid up with sickness, and when this able-looking, self-confident Wellgood presented himself for immediate employment, he took him out of hand with the merest glance at what looked like a very satisfactory reference. Later, he had intended to look up this reference, which he had been careful to preserve by sticking it, along with other papers, on his spike-file. But in the distractions following the untoward events of the evening, he had neglected to do so, feeling perfectly satisfied with the man's work and general behavior. Now it was a different thing. The man had left him summarily, and he felt impelled to hunt up the person who had recommended him and see whether this was the first time that Wellgood had repaid good treatment with bad. Running through the papers with which his file was now full, he found that the one he sought was not there. This roused him in good earnest, for he was certain that he had not removed it himself and there was no one else who had the right to do so. He suspected the culprit,—a young lad who occasionally had access to his desk. But this boy was no longer in the office. He had dismissed him for some petty fault the previous week, and it took him several days to find him again. Meantime his anger grew and when he finally came face to face with the lad, he accused him of the suspected trick with so much vehemence that the inevitable happened, and the boy confessed. This is what he acknowledged. He had taken the reference off the file, but only to give it to Wellgood himself, who had offered him money for it. When asked how much money, the boy admitted that the sum was ten dollars,—an extraordinary amount from a poor man for so simple a service, if the man merely wished to secure his reference for future use; so extraordinary that Mr. Jones grew more and more pertinent in his inquiries, eliciting finally what he surely could not have hoped for in the beginning,—the exact address of the party referred to in the paper he had stolen, and which, for some reason, the boy remembered. It was an uptown address, and, as soon as the caterer could leave his business, he took the elevated and proceeded to the specified street and number.

"Miss Van Arsdale, a surprise awaited him, and awaited us when he told the result of his search. The name attached to the recommendation had been—'Hiram Sears, Steward.' He did not know of any such man—perhaps you do—but when he reached the house from which the recommendation was dated, he saw that it was one of the great houses of New York, though he could not at the instant remember who lived there. But he soon found out. The first passer-by told him. Miss Van Arsdale, perhaps you can do the same. The number was—Eighty-sixth Street."

"—!" I repeated, quite aghast. "Why, Mr. Fairbrother himself! The husband of—"

"Exactly so, and Hiram Sears, whose name you may have heard mentioned at the inquest, though for a very good reason he was not there in person, is his steward and general factotum."

"Oh! and it was he who recommended Wellgood?"

"Yes."

"And did Mr. Jones see him?"

"No. The house, you remember, is closed. Mr. Fairbrother, on leaving town, gave his servants a vacation. His steward he took with him,—that is, they started together. But we hear no mention made of him in our telegrams from Santa Fe. He does not seem to have followed Mr. Fairbrother into the mountains."

"You say that in a peculiar way," I remarked.

"Because it has struck us peculiarly. Where is Sears now? And why did he not go on with Mr. Fairbrother when he left home with every apparent intention of accompanying him to the Placide mine? Miss Van Arsdale, we were impressed with this fact when we heard of Mr. Fairbrother's lonely trip from where he was taken ill to his mine outside of Santa Fe; but we have only given it its due importance since hearing what has come to us to-day.

"Miss Van Arsdale," continued the inspector, as I looked up quickly, "I am going to show great confidence in you. I am going to tell you what our men have learned about this Sears. As I have said before, it is but forestalling the reporters by a day, and it may help you to understand why I sent you such peremptory orders to stop, when your whole heart was fixed on an attempt by which you hoped to right Mr. Durand. We can not afford to disturb so distinguished a person as the one you have under your eye, while the least hope remains of fixing this crime elsewhere. And we have such hope. This man, this Sears, is by no means the simple character one would expect from his position. Considering the short time we have had (it was only yesterday that Jones found his way into this office), we have unearthed some very interesting facts in his regard. His devotion to Mr. Fairbrother was never any secret, and we knew as much about that the day after the murder as we do now. But the feelings with which he regarded Mrs. Fairbrother—well, that is another thing—and it was not till last night we heard that the attachment which bound him to her was of the sort which takes no account of youth or age, fitness or unfitness. He was no Adonis, and old enough, we are told, to be her father; but for all that we have already found several persons who can tell strange stories of the persistence with which his eager old eyes would follow her whenever chance threw them together during the time she remained under her husband's roof; and others who relate, with even more avidity, how, after her removal to apartments of her own, he used to spend hours in the adjoining park just to catch a glimpse of her figure as she crossed the sidewalk on her way to and from her carriage. Indeed, his senseless, almost senile passion for this magnificent beauty became a by-word in some mouths, and it only escaped being mentioned at the inquest from respect to Mr. Fairbrother, who had never recognized this weakness in his steward, and from its lack of visible connection with her horrible death and the stealing of her great jewel. Nevertheless, we have a witness now—it is astonishing how many witnesses we can scare up by a little effort, who never thought of coming forward themselves—who can swear to having seen him one night shaking his fist at her retreating figure as she stepped haughtily by him into her apartment house. This witness is sure that the man he saw thus gesticulating was Sears, and he is sure the woman was Mrs. Fairbrother. The only thing he is not sure of is how his own wife will feel when she hears that he was in that particular neighborhood on that particular evening, when he was evidently supposed to be somewhere else." And the inspector laughed.

"Is the steward's disposition a bad one." I asked, "that this display of feeling should impress you so much?"

"I don't know what to say about that yet. Opinions differ on this point. His friends speak of him as the mildest kind of a man who, without native executive skill, could not manage the great household he has in charge. His enemies, and we have unearthed a few, say, on the contrary, that they have never had any confidence in his quiet ways; that these were not in keeping with the fact or his having been a California miner in the early fifties.

"You can see I am putting you very nearly where we are ourselves. Nor do I see why I should not add that this passion of the seemingly subdued but really hot-headed steward for a woman, who never showed him anything but what he might call an insulting indifference, struck us as a clue to be worked up, especially after we received this answer to a telegram we sent late last night to the nurse who is caring for Mr. Fairbrother in New Mexico."

He handed me a small yellow slip and I read:

"The steward left Mr. Fairbrother at El Moro. He has not heard from him since.
"ANNETTA LA SERRA
"For Abner Fairbrother."

"At El Moro?" I cried. "Why, that was long enough ago."
"For him to have reached New York before the murder. Exactly so, if he took advantage of every close connection."

78

XIV. TRAPPED

I caught my breath sharply. I did not say anything. I felt that I did not understand the inspector sufficiently yet to speak. He seemed to be pleased with my reticence. At all events, his manner grew even kinder as he said:

"This Sears is a witness we must have. He is being looked for now, high and low, and we hope to get some clue to his whereabouts before night. That is, if he is in this city. Meanwhile, we are all glad—I am sure you are also—to spare so distinguished a gentleman as Mr. Grey the slightest annoyance."

"And Mr. Durand? What of him in this interim?"

"He will have to await developments. I see no other way, my dear."

It was kindly said, but my head drooped. This waiting was what was killing him and killing me. The inspector saw and gently patted my hand.

"Come," said he, "you have head enough to see that it is never wise to force matters." Then, possibly with an intention of rousing me, he remarked: "There is another small fact which may interest you. It concerns the waiter, Wellgood, recommended, as you will remember, by this Sears. In my talk with Jones it leaked out as a matter of small moment, and so it was to him, that this Wellgood was the waiter who ran and picked up the diamond after it fell from Mr. Grey's hand."

"Ah!"

"This may mean nothing—it meant nothing to Jones—but I inform you of it because there is a question I want to put to you in this connection. You smile."

"Did I?" I meekly answered. "I do not know why."

This was not true. I had been waiting to see why the inspector had so honored me with all these disclosures, almost with his thoughts. Now I saw. He desired something in return.

"You were on the scene at this very moment," he proceeded, after a brief contemplation of my face, "and you must have seen this man when he lifted the jewel and handed it back to Mr. Grey. Did you remark his features?"

"No, sir; I was too far off; besides, my eyes were on Mr. Grey." "That is a pity. I was in hopes you could satisfy me on a very important point."

"What point is that, Inspector Dalzell?"

"Whether he answered the following description." And, taking up another paper, he was about to read it aloud to me, when an interruption occurred. A man showed himself at the door, whom the inspector no sooner recognized than he seemed to forget me in his eagerness to interrogate him. Perhaps the appearance of the latter had something to do with it; he looked as if he had been running, or had been the victim of some extraordinary adventure. At all events, the inspector arose as he entered, and was about to question him when he remembered me, and, casting about for some means of ridding himself of my presence without injury to my feelings, he suddenly pushed open the door of an adjoining room and requested me to step inside while he talked a moment with this man.

Of course I went, but I cast him an appealing look as I did so. It evidently had its effect, for his expression changed as his band fell on the doorknob. Would he snap the lock tight, and so shut me out from what concerned me as much as it did any one in the whole world? Or would he recognize my anxiety— the necessity I was under of knowing just the ground I was standing on—and let me hear what this man had to report?

I watched the door. It closed slowly, too slowly to latch. Would he catch it anew by the knob? No; he left it thus, and, while the crack was hardly perceptible, I felt confident that the least shake of the floor would widen it and give me the opportunity I sought. But I did not have to wait for this. The two men in the office I had just left began to speak, and to my unbounded relief were sufficiently intelligible, even now, to warrant me in giving them my fullest attention.

After some expressions of astonishment on the part of the inspector as to the plight in which the other presented himself, the latter broke out:

"I've just escaped death! I'll tell you about that later. What I want to tell you now is that the man we want is in town. I saw him last night, or his shadow, which is the same thing. It was in the house in Eighty-sixth Street,—the house they all think closed. He came in with a key and—"

"Wait! You have him?"

"No. It's a long story, sir—"

"Tell it!"

The tone was dry. The inspector was evidently disappointed.

"Don't blame me till you hear," said the other. "He is no common crook. This is how it was: You wanted the suspect's photograph and a specimen of his writing. I knew no better place to look for them than in his own room in Mr. Fairbrother's house. I accordingly got the necessary warrant and late last evening undertook the job. I went alone I was always an egotistical chap, more's the pity—and with no further precaution than a passing explanation to the officer I met at the corner, I hastened up the block to the rear entrance on Eighty- seventh Street. There are three doors to the Fairbrother house, as you probably know. Two on Eighty-sixth Street (the large front one and a small one connecting directly with the turret stairs), and one on Eighty-seventh Street. It was to the latter I had a key. I do not think any one saw me go in. It was raining, and such people as went by were more concerned in keeping their umbrellas properly over their heads than in watching men skulking about in doorways.

"I got in, then, all right, and, being careful to close the door behind me, went up the first short flight of steps to what I knew must be the main hall. I had been given a plan of the interior, and I had studied it more or less before starting out, but I knew that I should get lost if I did not keep to the rear staircase, at the top of which I expected to find the steward's room. There was a faint light in the house, in spite of its closed shutters and tightly-drawn shades; and, having a certain dread of using my torch, knowing my weakness for pretty things and how hard it would be for me to pass so many fine rooms without looking in, I made my way up stairs, with no other guide than the hand-rail. When I had reached what I took to be the third floor I stopped. Finding it very dark, I first listened—a natural instinct with us—then I lit up and looked about me.

"I was in a large hall, empty as a vault and almost as desolate. Blank doors met my eyes in all directions, with here and there an open passageway. I felt myself in a maze. I had no idea which was the door I sought, and it is not pleasant to turn unaccustomed knobs in a shut-up house at midnight, with the rain pouring in torrents and the wind making pandemonium in a half-dozen great chimneys.

"But it had to be done, and I went at it in regular order till I came to a little narrow one opening on the turret-stair. This gave me my bearings. Sears' room adjoined the staircase. There was no difficulty in spotting the exact door now and, merely stopping to close the opening I had made to this little staircase, I crossed to this door and flung it open. I had been right in my calculations. It was the steward's room, and I made at once for the desk."

"And you found—?"

"Mostly locked drawers. But a key on my bunch opened some of these and my knife the rest. Here are the specimens of his handwriting which I collected. I doubt if you will get much out of them. I saw nothing compromising in the whole room, but then I hadn't time to go through his trunks, and one of them looked very interesting,—old as the hills and—"

"You hadn't time? Why hadn't you time? What happened to cut it short?"

"Well, sir, I'll tell you." The tone in which this was said roused me if it did not the inspector. "I had just come from the desk which had disappointed me, and was casting a look about the room, which was as bare as my hand of everything like ornament—I might almost say comfort—when I heard a noise which was not that of swishing rain or even gusty wind—these had not been absent from my ears for a moment. I didn't like that noise; it had a sneakish sound, and I shut my light off in a hurry. After that I crept hastily out of the room, for I don't like a set-to in a trap.

"It was darker than ever now in the hall, or so it seemed, and as I backed away I came upon a jog in the wall, behind which I crept. For the sound I had heard was no fancy. Some one besides myself was in the house, and that some one was coming up the little turret-stair, striking matches as he approached. Who could it be? A detective from the district attorney's office? I hardly thought so. He would have been provided with something better than matches to light his way. A burglar? No, not on the third floor of a house as rich as this. Some fellow on the force, then, who had seen me come in and, by some trick of his own, had managed to follow me? I would see. Meantime I kept my place behind the jog and watched, not knowing which way the intruder would go.

"Whoever he was, he was evidently astonished to see the turret door ajar, for he lit another match as he threw it open and, though I failed to get a glimpse of his figure, I succeeded in getting a very good one of his shadow. It was one to arouse a detective's instinct at once. I did not say to myself, this is the man I want, but I did say, this is nobody from headquarters, and I steadied myself for whatever might turn up.

"The first thing that happened was the sudden going out of the match which had made this shadow visible. The intruder did not light another. I heard him move across the floor with the rapid step of one who knows his way well, and the next minute a gas-jet flared up in the steward's room, and I knew that the man the whole force was looking for had trapped himself.

"You will agree that it was not my duty to take him then and there without seeing what he was after. He was thought to be in the eastern states, or south or west, and he was here; but why here? That is what I knew you would want to know, and it was just what I wanted to know myself. So I kept my place, which was good enough, and just listened, for I could not see.

"What was his errand? What did he want in this empty house at midnight? Papers first, and then clothes. I heard him at his desk, I heard him in the closet, and afterward pottering in the old trunk I had been so anxious to look into myself. He must have brought the key with him, for it was no time before I heard him throwing out the contents in a wild search for something he wanted in a great hurry. He found it sooner than you would believe, and began throwing the things back, when something happened. Expectedly or unexpectedly, his eye fell on some object which roused all his passions, and he broke into loud exclamations ending in groans. Finally he fell to kissing this object with a fervor suggesting rage, and a rage suggesting tenderness carried to the point of agony. I have never heard the like; my curiosity was so aroused that I was on the point of risking everything for a look, when he gave a sudden snarl and cried out, loud enough for me to hear: 'Kiss what I've hated? That is as bad as to kill what I've loved.' Those were the words. I am sure he said kiss and I am sure he said kill."

"This is very interesting. Go on with your story. Why didn't you collar him while he was in this mood? You would have won by the surprise.

"I had no pistol, sir, and he had. I heard him cock it. I thought he was going to take his own life, and held my breath for the report. But nothing like that was in his mind. Instead, he laid the pistol down and deliberately tore in two the object of his anger. Then with a smothered curse he made for the door and turret staircase.

"I was for following, but not till I had seen what he had destroyed in such an excess of feeling. I thought I knew, but I wanted to feel sure. So, before risking myself in the turret, I crept to the room he had left and felt about on the floor till I came upon these."

"A torn photograph! Mrs. Fairbrother's!"

"Yes. Have you not heard how he loved her? A foolish passion, but evidently sincere and—"

"Never mind comments, Sweetwater. Stick to facts."

"I will, sir. They are interesting enough. After I had picked up these scraps I stole back to the turret staircase. And here I made my first break. I stumbled in the darkness, and the man below heard me, for the pistol clicked again. I did not like this, and had some thoughts of backing out of my job. But I didn't. I merely waited till I heard his step again; then I followed.

"But very warily this time. It was not an agreeable venture. It was like descending into a well with possible death at the bottom. I could see nothing and presently could hear nothing but the almost imperceptible sliding of my own fingers down the curve of the wall, which was all I had to guide me. Had he stopped midway, and would my first intimation of his presence be the touch of cold steel or the flinging around me of two murderous arms? I had met with no break in the smooth surface of the wall, so could not have reached the second story. When I should get there the question would be whether to leave the staircase and seek him in the mazes of its great rooms, or to keep on down to the parlor floor and so to the street, whither he was possibly bound. I own that I was almost tempted to turn on my light and have done with it, but I remembered of how little use I should be to you lying in this well of a stairway with a bullet in me, and so I managed to compose myself and go on as I had begun. Next instant my fingers slipped round the edge of an opening, and I knew that the moment of decision had come. Realizing that no one can move so softly that he will not give away his presence in some way, I paused for the sound which I knew must come, and when a click rose from the depths of the hall before me I plunged into that hall and thus into the house proper.

"Here it was not so dark; yet I could make out none of the objects I now and then ran against. I passed a mirror (I hardly know how I knew it to be such), and in that mirror I seemed to see the ghost of a ghost flit by and vanish. It was too much. I muttered a suppressed oath and plunged forward, when I struck against a closing door. It flew open again and I rushed in, turning on my light in my extreme desperation, when, instead of hearing the sharp report of a pistol, as I expected, I saw a second door fall to before me, this time with a sound like the snap of a spring lock. Finding that this was so, and that all advance was barred that way, I wheeled hurriedly back toward the door by which I had entered the place, to find that that had fallen to simultaneously with the other, a single spring acting for both. I was trapped—a prisoner in the strangest sort of passageway or closet; and, as a speedy look about presently assured me, a prisoner with very little hope of immediate escape, for the doors were not only immovable, without even locks to pick or panels to break in, but the place was bare of windows, and the only communication which it could be said to have with the outside world at all was a shaft rising from the ceiling almost to the top of the house. Whether this served as a ventilator, or a means of lighting up the hole when both doors were shut, it was much too inaccessible to offer any apparent way of escape.

"Never was a man more thoroughly boxed in. As I realized how little chance there was of any outside interference, how my captor, even if he was seen leaving the house by the officer on duty, would be taken for myself and so allowed to escape, I own that I felt my position a hopeless one. But anger is a powerful stimulant, and I was mortally angry, not only with Sears, but with myself. So when I was done swearing I took another look around, and, finding that there was no getting through the walls, turned my attention wholly to the shaft, which would certainly lead me out of the place if I could only find means to mount it.

"And how do you think I managed to do this at last? A look at my bedraggled, lime-covered clothes may give you some idea. I cut a passage for myself up those perpendicular walls as the boy did up the face of the natural bridge in Virginia. Do you remember that old story in the Reader? It came to me like an inspiration as I stood looking up from below, and though I knew that I should have to work most of the way in perfect darkness, I decided that a man's life was worth some risk, and that I had rather fall and break my neck while doing something than to spend hours in maddening inactivity, only to face death at last from slow starvation.

"I had a knife, an exceedingly good knife, in my pocket—and for the first few steps I should have the light of my electric torch. The difficulty (that is, the first difficulty) was to reach the shaft from the floor where I stood. There was but one article of furniture in the room, and that was something between a table and a desk. No chairs, and the desk was not high enough to enable me to reach the mouth of the shaft. If I could turn it on end there might be some hope. But this did not look feasible. However, I threw off my coat and went at the thing with a vengeance, and whether I was given superhuman power or whether the clumsy thing was not as heavy as it looked, I did finally succeed in turning it on its end close under the opening from which the shaft rose. The next thing was to get on its top. That seemed about as impossible as climbing the bare wall itself, but presently I bethought me of the drawers, and, though they were locked, I did succeed by the aid of my keys to get enough of them open to make for myself a very good pair of stairs.

"I could now see my way to the mouth of the shaft, but after that! Taking out my knife, I felt the edge. It was a good one, so was the point, but was it good enough to work holes in plaster? It depended somewhat upon the plaster. Had the masons, in finishing that shaft, any thought of the poor wretch who one day would have to pit his life against the hardness of the final covering? My first dig at it would tell. I own I trembled violently at the prospect of what that first test would mean to me, and wondered if the perspiration which I felt starting at every pore was the result of the effort I had been engaged in or just plain fear.

"Inspector, I do not intend to have you live with me through the five mortal hours which followed. I was enabled to pierce that plaster with my knife, and even to penetrate deep enough to afford a place for the tips of my fingers and afterward for the point of my toes, digging, prying, sweating, panting, listening, first for a sudden opening of the doors beneath, then for some shout or wicked interference from above as I worked my way up inch by inch, foot by foot, to what might not be safety after it was attained.

"Five hours—six. Then I struck something which proved to be a window; and when I realized this and knew that with but one more effort I should breathe freely again, I came as near falling as I had at any time before I began this terrible climb.

"Happily, I had some premonition of my danger, and threw myself into a position which held me till the dizzy minute passed. Then I went calmly on with my work, and in another half-hour had reached the window, which, fortunately for me, not only opened inward, but was off the latch. It was with a sense of inexpressible relief that I clambered through this window and for a brief moment breathed in the pungent odor of cedar. But it could have been only for a moment. It was three o'clock in the afternoon before I found myself again in the outer air. The only way I can account for the lapse of time is that the strain to which both body and nerve had been subjected was too much for even my hardy body and that I fell to the floor of the cedar closet and from a faint went into a sleep that lasted until two. I can easily account for the last hour because it took me that long to cut the thick paneling from the door of the closet. However, I am here now, sir, and in very much the same condition in which I left that house. I thought my first duty was to tell you that I had seen Hiram Sears in that house last night and put you on his track."

I drew a long breath,—I think the inspector did. I had been almost rigid from excitement, and I don't believe he was quite free from it either. But his voice was calmer than I expected when he finally said:

"I'll remember this. It was a good night's work." Then the inspector put to him some questions, which seemed to fix the fact that Sears had left the house before Sweetwater did, after which he bade him send certain men to him and then go and fix himself up.

I believe he had forgotten me. I had almost forgotten myself.

XV. SEARS OR WELLGOOD

Not till the inspector had given several orders was I again summoned into his presence. He smiled as our eyes met, but did not allude, any more than I did, to what had just passed. Nevertheless, we understood each other.

When I was again seated, he took up the conversation where we had left it.

"The description I was just about to read to you," he went on; "will you listen to it now?"

"Gladly," said I; "it is Wellgood's, I believe."

He did not answer save by a curious glance from under his brows, but, taking the paper again from his desk, went on reading:

"A man of fifty-five looking like one of sixty. Medium height, insignificant features, head bald save for a ring of scanty dark hair. No beard, a heavy nose, long mouth and sleepy half-shut eyes capable of shooting strange glances. Nothing distinctive in face or figure save the depth of his wrinkles and a scarcely observable stoop in his right shoulder. Do you see Wellgood in that?" he suddenly asked.

"I have only the faintest recollection of his appearance," was my doubtful reply. "But the impression I get from this description is not exactly the one I received of that waiter in the momentary glimpse I got of him."

"So others have told me before;" he remarked, looking very disappointed. "The description is of Sears given me by a man who knew him well, and if we could fit the description of the one to that of the other, we should have it easy. But the few persons who have seen Wellgood differ greatly in their remembrance of his features, and even of his coloring. It is astonishing how superficially most people see a man, even when they are thrown into daily contact with him. Mr. Jones says the man's eyes are gray, his hair a wig and dark, his nose pudgy, and his face without much expression. His land-lady, that his eyes are blue, his hair, whether wig or not, a dusty auburn, and his look quick and piercing,—a look which always made her afraid. His nose she don't remember. Both agree, or rather all agree, that he wore no beard—Sears did, but a beard can be easily taken off—and all of them declare that they would know him instantly if they saw him. And so the matter stands. Even you can give me no definite description,—one, I mean, as satisfactory or unsatisfactory as this of Sears."

I shook my head. Like the others, I felt that I should know him if I saw him, but I could go no further than that. There seemed to be so little that was distinctive about the man.

The inspector, hoping, perhaps, that all this would serve to rouse my memory, shrugged his shoulders and put the best face he could on the matter.

"Well, well," said he, "we shall have to be patient. A day may make all the difference possible in our outlook. If we can lay hands on either of these men—"

He seemed to realize he had said a word too much, for he instantly changed the subject by asking if I had succeeded in getting a sample of Miss Grey's writing. I was forced to say no; that everything had been very carefully put away. "But I do not know what moment I may come upon it," I added. "I do not forget its importance in this investigation."

"Very good. Those lines handed up to Mrs. Fairbrother from the walk outside are the second most valuable clue we possess."

I did not ask him what the first was. I knew. It was the stiletto.

"Strange that no one has testified to that handwriting," I remarked.

He looked at me in surprise.

"Fifty persons have sent in samples of writing which they think like it," he observed. "Often of persons who never heard of the Fairbrothers. We have been bothered greatly with the business. You know little of the difficulties the police labor under."

"I know too much," I sighed.

He smiled and patted me on the hand.

"Go back to your patient," he said. "Forget every other duty but that of your calling until you get some definite word from me. I shall not keep you in suspense one minute longer than is absolutely necessary."

He had risen. I rose too. But I was not satisfied. I could not leave the room with my ideas (I might say with my convictions) in such a turmoil.

"Inspector," said I, "you will think me very obstinate, but all you have told me about Sears, all I have heard about him, in fact,"—this I emphasized,—"does not convince me of the entire folly of my own suspicions. Indeed, I am afraid that, if anything, they are strengthened. This steward, who is a doubtful character, I acknowledge, may have had his reasons for wishing Mrs. Fairbrother's death, may even have had a hand in the matter; but what evidence have you to show that he, himself, entered the alcove, struck the blow or stole the diamond? I have listened eagerly for some such evidence, but I have listened in vain."

"I know," he murmured, "I know. But it will come; at least I think so."

This should have reassured me, no doubt, and sent me away quiet and happy. But something—the tenacity of a deep conviction, possibly—kept me lingering before the inspector and finally gave me the courage to say:

"I know I ought not to speak another word; that I am putting myself at a disadvantage in doing so; but I can not help it, Inspector; I can not help it when I see you laying such stress upon the few indirect clues connecting the suspicious Sears with this crime, and ignoring the direct clues we have against one whom we need not name."

Had I gone too far? Had my presumption transgressed all bounds and would he show a very natural anger? No, he smiled instead, an enigmatical smile, no doubt, which I found it difficult to understand, but yet a smile.

"You mean," he suggested, "that Sears' possible connection with the crime can not eliminate Mr. Grey's very positive one; nor can the fact that Wellgood's hand came in contact with Mr. Grey's, at or near the time of the exchange of the false stone with the real, make it any less evident who was the guilty author of this exchange?"

The inspector's hand was on the door-knob, but he dropped it at this, and surveying me very quietly said:

"I thought that a few days spent at the bedside of Miss Grey in the society of so renowned and cultured a gentleman as her father would disabuse you of these damaging suspicions."

"I don't wonder that you thought so," I burst out. "You would think so all the more, if you knew how kind he can be and what solicitude he shows for all about him. But I can not get over the facts. They all point, it seems to me, straight in one direction."

"All? You heard what was said in this room—I saw it in your eye—how the man, who surprised the steward in his own room last night, heard him talking of love and death in connection with Mrs. Fairbrother. 'To kiss what I hate! It is almost as bad as to kill what I love'—he said something like that."

"Yes, I heard that. But did he mean that he had been her actual slayer? Could you convict him on those words?"

"Well, we shall find out. Then, as to Wellgood's part in the little business, you choose to consider that it took place at the time the stone fell from Mr. Grey's hand. What proof have you that the substitution you believe in was not made by him? He could easily have done it while crossing the room to Mr. Grey's side."

"Inspector!" Then hotly, as the absurdity of the suggestion struck me with full force: "He do this! A waiter, or as you think, Mr. Fairbrother's steward, to be provided with so hard-to-come-by an article as this counterpart of a great stone? Isn't that almost as incredible a supposition as any I have myself presumed to advance?"

"Possibly, but the affair is full of incredibilities, the greatest of which, to my mind, is the persistence with which you, a kind-hearted enough little woman, persevere in ascribing the deepest guilt to one you profess to admire and certainly would be glad to find innocent of any complicity with a great crime."

I felt that I must justify myself.

"Mr. Durand has had no such consideration shown him," said I.

"I know, my child, I know; but the cases differ. Wouldn't it be well for you to see this and be satisfied with the turn which things have taken, without continuing to insist upon involving Mr. Grey in your suspicions?"

A smile took off the edge of this rebuke, yet I felt it keenly; and only the confidence I had in his fairness as a man and public official enabled me to say:

"But I am talking quite confidentially. And you have been so good to me, so willing to listen to all I had to say, that I can not help but speak my whole mind. It is my only safety valve. Remember how I have to sit in the presence of this man with my thoughts all choked up. It is killing me. But I think I should go back content if you will listen to one more suggestion I have to make. It is my last."

"Say it I am nothing if not indulgent."

He had spoken the word. Indulgent, that was it. He let me speak, probably had let me speak from the first, from pure kindness. He did not believe one little bit in my good sense or logic. But I was not to be deterred. I would empty my mind of the ugly thing that lay there. I would leave there no miserable dregs of doubt to ferment and work their evil way with me in the dead watches of the night, which I had yet to face. So I took him at his word.

"I only want to ask this. In case Sears is innocent of the crime, who wrote the warning and where did the assassin get the stiletto with the Grey arms chased into its handle? And the diamond? Still the diamond! You hint that he stole that, too. That with some idea of its proving useful to him on this gala occasion, he had provided himself with an imitation stone, setting and all,—he who has never shown, so far as we have heard, any interest in Mrs. Fairbrother's diamond, only in Mrs. Fairbrother herself. If Wellgood is Sears and Sears the medium by which the false stone was exchanged for the real, then he made this exchange in Mr. Grey's interests and not his own. But I don't believe he had anything to do with it. I think everything goes to show that the exchange was made by Mr. Grey himself."

"A second Daniel," muttered the inspector lightly. "Go on, little lawyer!" But for all this attempt at banter on his part, I imagined that I saw the beginning of a very natural anxiety to close the conversation. I therefore hastened with what I had yet to say, cutting my words short and almost stammering in my eagerness.

"Remember the perfection of that imitation stone, a copy so exact that it extends to the setting. That shows plan—forgive me if I repeat myself— preparation, a knowledge of stones, a particular knowledge of this one. Mr. Fairbrother's steward may have had the knowledge, but he would have been a fool to have used his knowledge to secure for himself a valuable he could never have found a purchaser for in any market. But a fancier—one who has his pleasure in the mere possession of a unique and invaluable gem—ah! that is different! He might risk a crime—history tells us of several."

Here I paused to take breath, which gave the inspector chance to say:

"In other words, this is what you think. The Englishman, desirous of covering up his tracks, conceived the idea of having this imitation on hand, in case it might be of use in the daring and disgraceful undertaking you ascribe to him. Recognizing his own inability to do this himself, he delegated the task to one who in some way, he had been led to think, cherished a secret grudge against its present possessor—a man who had had some opportunity for seeing the stone and studying the setting. The copy thus procured, Mr. Grey went to the ball, and, relying on his own seemingly unassailable position, attacked Mrs. Fairbrother in the alcove and would have carried off the diamond, if he had found it where he had seen it earlier blazing on her breast. But it was not there. The warning received by her—a warning you ascribe to his daughter, a fact which is yet to be proved—had led her to rid herself of the jewel in the way Mr. Durand describes, and he found himself burdened with a dastardly crime and with nothing to show for it. Later, however, to his intense surprise and possible satisfaction, he saw that diamond in my hands, and, recognizing an opportunity, as he thought, of yet securing it, he asked to see it, held it for an instant, and then, making use of an almost incredible expedient for distracting attention, dropped, not the real stone but the false one, retaining the real one in his hand. This, in plain English, as I take it, is your present idea of the situation."

Astonished at the clearness with which he read my mind, I answered: "Yes, Inspector, that is what was in my mind."

"Good! then it is just as well that it is out. Your mind is now free and you can give it entirely to your duties." Then, as he laid his hand on the door-knob, he added: "In studying so intently your own point of view, you seem to have forgotten that the last thing which Mr. Grey would be likely to do, under those circumstances, would be to call attention to the falsity of the gem upon whose similarity to the real stone he was depending. Not even his confidence in his own position, as an honored and highly-esteemed guest, would lead him to do that."

"Not if he were a well-known connoisseur," I faltered, "with the pride of one who has handled the best gems? He would know that the deception would be soon discovered and that it would not do for him to fail to recognize it for what it was, when the make-believe was in his hands."

"Forced, my dear child, forced; and as chimerical as all the rest. It can not stand putting into words. I will go further,—you are a good girl and can bear to hear the truth from me. I don't believe in your theory; I can't. I have not been able to from the first, nor have any of my men; but if your ideas are true and Mr. Grey is involved in this matter, you will find that there has been more of a hitch about that diamond than you, in your simplicity, believe. If Mr. Grey were in actual possession of this valuable, he would show less care than you say he does. So would he if it were in Wellgood's hands with his consent and a good prospect of its coming to him in the near future. But if it is in Wellgood's hands without his consent, or any near prospect of his regaining it, then we can easily understand his present apprehensions and the growing uneasiness he betrays."

"True," I murmured.

"If, then," the inspector pursued, giving me a parting glance not without its humor, probably not without something really serious underlying its humor, "we should find, in following up our present clue, that Mr. Grey has had dealings with this Wellgood or this Sears; or if you, with your advantages for learning the fact, should discover that he shows any extraordinary interest in either of them, the matter will take on a different aspect. But we have not got that far yet. At present our task is to find one or the other of these men. If we are lucky, we shall discover that the waiter and the steward are identical, in spite of their seemingly different appearance. A rogue, such as this Sears has shown himself to be, would be an adept at disguise."

"You are right," I acknowledged. "He has certainly the heart of a criminal. If he had no hand in Mrs. Fairbrother's murder, he came near having one in that of your detective. You know what I mean. I could not help hearing, Inspector."

He smiled, looked me steadfastly in the face for a moment, and then bowed me out.

The inspector told me afterward that, in spite of the cavalier manner with which he had treated my suggestions, he spent a very serious half-hour, head to head with the district attorney. The result was the following order to Sweetwater, the detective.

"You are to go to the St. Regis; make yourself solid there, and gradually, as you can manage it, work yourself into a position for knowing all that goes on in Room ——. If the gentleman (mind you, the gentleman; we care nothing about the women) should go out, you are to follow him if it takes you to——. We want to know his secret; but he must never know our interest in it and you are to be as silent in this matter as if possessed of neither ear nor tongue. I will add memory, for if you find this secret to be one in which we have no lawful interest, you are to forget it absolutely and for ever. You will understand why when you consult the St Regis register."

But they expected nothing from it; absolutely nothing.

XVI. DOUBT

I prayed uncle that we might be driven home by the way of Eighty-sixth Street. I wanted to look at the Fairbrother house. I had seen it many times, but I felt that I should see it with new eyes after the story I had just heard in the inspector's office. That an adventure of this nature could take place in a New York house taxed my credulity. I might have believed it of Paris, wicked, mysterious Paris, the home of intrigue and every redoubtable crime, but of our own homely, commonplace metropolis—the house must be seen for me to be convinced of the fact related.

Many of you know the building. It is usually spoken of with a shrug, the sole reason for which seems to be that there is no other just like it in the city. I myself have always considered it imposing and majestic; but to the average man it is too suggestive of Old-World feudal life to be pleasing. On this afternoon—a dull, depressing one—it looked undeniably heavy as we approached it; but interesting in a very new way to me, because of the great turret at one angle, the scene of that midnight descent of two men, each in deadly fear of the other, yet quailing not in their purpose,—the one of flight, the other of pursuit.

There was no railing in front of the house. It may have seemed an unnecessary safeguard to the audacious owner. Consequently, the small door in the turret opened directly upon the street, making entrance and exit easy enough for any one who had the key. But the shaft and the small room at the bottom— where were they? Naturally in the center of the great mass, the room being without windows.

It was, therefore, useless to look for it, and yet my eye ran along the peaks and pinnacles of the roof, searching for the skylight in which it undoubtedly ended. At last I espied it, and, my curiosity satisfied on this score, I let my eyes run over the side and face of the building for an open window or a lifted shade. But all were tightly closed and gave no more sign of life than did the boarded-up door. But I was not deceived by this. As we drove away, I thought how on the morrow there would be a regular procession passing through this street to see just the little I had seen to-day. The detective's adventure was like to make the house notorious. For several minutes after I had left its neighborhood my imagination pictured room after room shut up from the light of day, but bearing within them the impalpable aura of those two shadows flitting through them like the ghosts of ghosts, as the detective had tellingly put it.

The heart has its strange surprises. Through my whole ride and the indulgence in these thoughts I was conscious of a great inner revulsion against all I had intimated and even honestly felt while talking with the inspector. Perhaps this is what this wise old official expected. He had let me talk, and the inevitable reaction followed. I could now see only Mr. Grey's goodness and claims to respect, and began to hate myself that I had not been immediately impressed by the inspector's views, and shown myself more willing to drop every suspicion against the august personage I had presumed to associate with crime. What had given me the strength to persist? Loyalty to my lover? His innocence had not been involved. Indeed, every word uttered in the inspector's office had gone to prove that he no longer occupied a leading place in police calculations: that their eyes were turned elsewhere, and that I had only to be patient to see Mr. Durand quite cleared in their minds.

But was this really so? Was he as safe as that? What if this new clue failed? What if they failed to find Sears or lay hands on the doubtful Wellgood? Would Mr. Durand be released without a trial? Should we hear nothing more of the strange and to many the suspicious circumstances which linked him to this crime? It would be expecting too much from either police or official discrimination.

No; Mr. Durand would never be completely exonerated till the true culprit was found and all explanations made. I had therefore been simply fighting his battles when I pointed out what I thought to be the weak place in their present theory, and, sore as I felt in contemplation of my seemingly heartless action, I was not the unimpressionable, addle-pated nonentity I must have seemed to the inspector.

Yet my comfort was small and the effort it took to face Mr. Grey and my young patient was much greater than I had anticipated. I blushed as I approached to take my place at Miss Grey's bedside, and, had her father been as suspicious of me at that moment as I was of him, I am sure that I should have fared badly in his thoughts.

But he was not on the watch for my emotions. He was simply relieved to see me back. I noticed this immediately, also that something had occurred during my absence which absorbed his thought and filled him with anxiety.

A Western Union envelope lay at his feet,—proof that he had just received a telegram. This, under ordinary circumstances, would not have occasioned me a second thought, such a man being naturally the recipient of all sorts of communications from all parts of the world; but at this crisis, with the worm of a half-stifled doubt still gnawing at my heart, everything that occurred to him took on importance and roused questions.

When he had left the room, Miss Grey nestled up to me with the seemingly ingenuous remark:

"Poor papa! something disturbs him. He will not tell me what. I suppose he thinks I am not strong enough to share his troubles. But I shall be soon. Don't you see I am gaining every day?"

"Indeed I do," was my hearty response. In face of such a sweet confidence and open affection doubt vanished and I was able to give all my thoughts to her.

"I wish papa felt as sure of this as you do," she said. "For some reason he does not seem to take any comfort from my improvement. When Doctor Freligh says, 'Well, well! we are getting on finely to-day,' I notice that he does not look less anxious, nor does he even meet these encouraging words with a smile. Haven't you noticed it? He looks as care-worn and troubled about me now as he did the first day I was taken sick. Why should he? Is it because he has lost so many children he can not believe in his good fortune at having the most insignificant of all left to him?"

"I do not know your father very well," I protested; "and can not judge what is going on in his mind. But he must see that you are quite a different girl from what you were a week ago, and that, if nothing unforeseen happens, your recovery will only be a matter of a week or two longer."

"Oh, how I love to hear you say that! To be well again! To read letters!" she murmured, "and to write them!" And I saw the delicate hand falter up to pinch the precious packet awaiting that happy hour. I did not like to discuss her father with her, so took this opportunity to turn the conversation aside into safer channels. But we had not proceeded far before Mr. Grey returned and, taking his stand at the foot of the bed, remarked, after a moment's gloomy contemplation of his daughter's face:

"You are better today, the doctor says,—I have just been telephoning to him. But do you feel well enough for me to leave you for a few days? There is a man I must see—must go to, if you have no dread of being left alone with your good nurse and the doctor's constant attendance."

Miss Grey looked startled. Doubtless she found it difficult to understand what man in this strange country could interest her father enough to induce him to leave her while he was yet laboring under such solicitude. But a smile speedily took the place of her look of surprised inquiry and she affectionately exclaimed:

"Oh, I haven't the least dread in the world, not now. See, I can hold up my arms. Go, papa, go; it will give me a chance to surprise you with my good looks when you come back."

He turned abruptly away. He was suffering from an emotion deeper than he cared to acknowledge. But he gained control over himself speedily and, coming back, announced with forced decision:

"I shall have to go to-night. I have no choice. Promise me that you will not go back in my absence; that you will strive to get well; that you will put all your mind into striving to get well."

"Indeed, I will," she answered, a little frightened by the feeling he showed. "Don't worry so much. I have more than one reason for living, papa."

He shook his head and went immediately to make his preparations for departure. His daughter gave one sob, then caught me by the hand.

"You look dumfounded," said she. "But never mind, we shall get on very well together. I have the most perfect confidence in you."

Was it my duty to let the inspector know that Mr. Grey anticipated absenting himself from the city for a few days? I decided that I would only be impressing my own doubts upon him after a rebuke which should have allayed them.

Yet, when Mr. Grey came to take his departure I wished that the inspector might have been a witness to his emotion, if only to give me one of his very excellent explanations. The parting was more like that of one who sees no immediate promise of return than of a traveler who intends to limit his stay to a few days. He looked her in the eyes and kissed her a dozen times, each time with an air of heartbreak which was good neither for her nor for himself, and when he finally tore himself away it was to look back at her from the door with an expression I was glad she did not see, or it would certainly have interfered with the promise she had made to concentrate all her energies on getting well.

What was at the root of his extreme grief at leaving her? Did he fear the person he was going to meet, or were his plans such as involved a much longer stay than he had mentioned? Did he even mean to return at all?

Ah, that was the question! Did he intend to return, or had I been the unconscious witness of a flight?

XVII. SWEETWATER IN A NEW ROLE

A few days later three men were closeted in the district attorney's office. Two of them were officials—the district attorney himself, and our old friend, the inspector. The third was the detective, Sweetwater, chosen by them to keep watch on Mr. Grey.

Sweetwater had just come to town,—this was evident from the gripsack he had set down in a corner on entering, also from a certain tousled appearance which bespoke hasty rising and but few facilities for proper attention to his person. These details counted little, however, in the astonishment created by his manner. For a hardy chap he looked strangely nervous and indisposed, so much so that, after the first short greeting, the inspector asked him what was up, and if he had had another Fairbrother-house experience.

He replied with a decided no; that it was not his adventure which had upset him, but the news he had to bring.

Here he glanced at every door and window; and then, leaning forward over the table at which the two officials sat, he brought his head as nearly to them as possible and whispered five words.

They produced a most unhappy sensation. Both the men, hardened as they were by duties which soon sap the sensibilities, started and turned as pale as the speaker himself. Then the district attorney, with one glance at the inspector, rose and locked the door.

It was a prelude to this tale which I give, not as it came from his mouth, but as it was afterward related to me. The language, I fear, is mostly my own.

The detective had just been with Mr. Grey to the coast of Maine. Why there, will presently appear. His task had been to follow this gentleman, and follow him he did.

Mr. Grey was a very stately man, difficult of approach, and was absorbed, besides, by some overwhelming care. But this fellow was one in a thousand and somehow, during the trip, he managed to do him some little service, which drew the attention of the great man to himself. This done, he so improved his opportunity that the two were soon on the best of terms, and he learned that the Englishman was without a valet, and, being unaccustomed to move about without one, felt the awkwardness of his position very much. This gave Sweetwater his cue, and when he found that the services of such a man were wanted only during the present trip and for the handling of affairs quite apart from personal tendance upon the gentleman himself, he showed such an honest desire to fill the place, and made out to give such a good account of himself, that he found himself engaged for the work before reaching C—.

This was a great stroke of luck, he thought, but he little knew how big a stroke or into what a series of adventures it was going to lead him.

Once on the platform of the small station at which Mr. Grey had bidden him to stop, he noticed two things: the utter helplessness of the man in all practical matters, and his extreme anxiety to see all that was going on about him without being himself seen. There was method in this curiosity, too much method. Women did not interest him in the least. They could pass and repass without arousing his attention, but the moment a man stepped his way, he shrank from him only to betray the greatest curiosity concerning him the moment he felt it safe to turn and observe him. All of which convinced Sweetwater that the Englishman's errand was in connection with a man whom he equally dreaded and desired to meet.

Of this he was made absolutely certain a little later. As they were leaving the depot with the rest of the arrivals, Mr. Grey said:

"I want you to get me a room at a very quiet hotel. This done, you are to hunt up the man whose name you will find written in this paper, and when you have found him, make up your mind how it will be possible for me to get a good look at him without his getting any sort of a look at me. Do this and you will earn a week's salary in one day."

Sweetwater, with his head in air and his heart on fire—for matters were looking very promising indeed—took the paper and put it in his pocket; then he began to hunt for a hotel. Not till he had found what he wished, and installed the Englishman in his room, did he venture to open the precious memorandum and read the name he had been speculating over for an hour. It was not the one he had anticipated, but it came near to it. It was that of James Wellgood.

Satisfied now that he had a ticklish matter to handle, he prepared for it, with his usual enthusiasm and circumspection.

Sauntering out into the street, he strolled first toward the post-office. The train on which he had just come had been a mail-train, and he calculated that he would find half the town there.

His calculation was a correct one. The store was crowded with people. Taking his place in the line drawn up before the post-office window, he awaited his turn, and when it came shouted out the name which was his one talisman— James Wellgood.

The man behind the boxes was used to the name and reached out a hand toward a box unusually well stacked, but stopped half-way there and gave Sweetwater a sharp look.

"Who are you?" he asked.

"A stranger," that young man put in volubly, "looking for James Wellgood. I thought, perhaps, you could tell me where to find him. I see that his letters pass through this office."

"You're taking up another man's time," complained the postmaster. He probably alluded to the man whose elbow Sweetwater felt boring into his back. "Ask Dick over there; he knows him."

The detective was glad enough to escape and ask Dick. But he was better pleased yet when Dick—a fellow with a squint whose hand was always in the sugar—told him that Mr. Wellgood would probably be in for his mail in a few moments. "That is his buggy standing before the drug-store on the opposite side of the way."

So! he had netted Jones' quondam waiter at the first cast! "Lucky!" was what he said to himself, "still lucky!"

Sauntering to the door, he watched for the owner of that buggy. He had learned, as such fellows do, that there was a secret hue and cry after this very man by the New York police; that he was supposed by some to be Sears himself. In this way he would soon be looking upon the very man whose steps he had followed through the Fairbrother house a few nights before, and through whose resolute action he had very nearly run the risk of a lingering death from starvation.

"A dangerous customer," thought he. "I wonder if my instinct will go so far as to make me recognize his presence. I shouldn't wonder. It has served me almost as well as that many times before."

It appeared to serve him now, for when the man finally showed himself on the cross-walk separating the two buildings he experienced a sudden indecision not unlike that of dread, and there being nothing in the man's appearance to warrant apprehension, he took it for the instinctive recognition it undoubtedly was.

He therefore watched him narrowly and succeeded in getting one glance from his eye. It was enough. The man was commonplace,—commonplace in feature, dress and manner, but his eye gave him away. There was nothing commonplace in that. It was an eye to beware of.

He had taken in Sweetwater as he passed, but Sweetwater was of a commonplace type, too, and woke no corresponding dread in the other's mind; for he went whistling into the store, from which he presently reissued with a bundle of mail in his hand. The detective's first instinct was to take him into custody as a suspect much wanted by the New York police; but reason assured him that he not only had no warrant for this, but that he would better serve the ends of justice by following out his present task of bringing this man and the Englishman together and watching the result. But how, with the conditions laid on him by Mr. Grey, was this to be done? He knew nothing of the man's circumstances or of his position in the town. How, then, go to work to secure his cooperation in a scheme possibly as mysterious to him as it was to himself? He could stop this stranger in mid-street, with some plausible excuse, but it did not follow that he would succeed in luring him to the hotel where Mr. Grey could see him. Wellgood, or, as he believed, Sears, knew too much of life to be beguiled by any open clap-trap, and Sweetwater was obliged to see him drive off without having made the least advance in the purpose engrossing him.

But that was nothing. He had all the evening before him, and reentering the store, he took up his stand near the sugar barrel. He had perceived that in the pauses of weighing and tasting, Dick talked; if he were guided with suitable discretion, why should he not talk of Wellgood?

He was guided, and he did talk and to some effect. That is, he gave information of the man which surprised Sweetwater. If in the past and in New York he had been known as a waiter, or should I say steward, he was known here as a manufacturer of patent medicine designed to rejuvenate the human race. He had not been long in town and was somewhat of a stranger yet, but he wouldn't be so long. He was going to make things hum, he was. Money for this, money for that, a horse where another man would walk, and mail—well, that alone would make this post-office worth while. Then the drugs ordered by wholesale. Those boxes over there were his, ready to be carted out to his manufactory. Count them, some one, and think of the bottles and bottles of stuff they stand for. If it sells as he says it will—then he will soon be rich: and so on, till Sweetwater brought the garrulous Dick to a standstill by asking whether Wellgood had been away for any purpose since he first came to town. He received the reply that he had just come home from New York, where he had been for some articles needed in his manufactory. Sweetwater felt all his convictions confirmed, and ended the colloquy with the final question:

"And where is his manufactory? Might be worth visiting, perhaps."

The other made a gesture, said something about northwest and rushed to help a customer. Sweetwater took the opportunity to slide away. More explicit directions could easily be got elsewhere, and he felt anxious to return to Mr. Grey and discover, if possible, whether it would prove as much a matter of surprise to him as to Sweetwater himself that the man who answered to the name of Wellgood was the owner of a manufactory and a barrel or two of drugs, out of which he proposed to make a compound that would rob the doctors of their business and make himself and this little village rich.

Sweetwater made only one stop on his way to Mr. Grey's hotel rooms, and that was at the stables. Here he learned whatever else there was to know, and, armed with definite information, he appeared before Mr. Grey, who, to his astonishment, was dining in his own room.

He had dismissed the waiter and was rather brooding than eating. He looked up eagerly, however, when Sweetwater entered, and asked what news.

The detective, with some semblance of respect, answered that he had seen Wellgood, but that he had been unable to detain him or bring him within his employer's observation.

"He is a patent-medicine man," he then explained, "and manufactures his own concoctions in a house he has rented here on a lonely road some half-mile out of town."

"Wellgood does? the man named Wellgood?" Mr. Grey exclaimed with all the astonishment the other secretly expected.

"Yes; Wellgood, James Wellgood. There is no other in town."

"How long has this man been here?" the statesman inquired, after a moment of apparently great discomfiture.

"Just twenty-four hours, this time. He was here once before, when he rented the house and made all his plans."

"Ah!"

Mr. Grey rose precipitately. His manner had changed.

"I must see him. What you tell me makes it all the more necessary for me to see him. How can you bring it about?"

"Without his seeing you?" Sweetwater asked.

"Yes, yes; certainly without his seeing me. Couldn't you rap him up at his own door, and hold him in talk a minute, while I looked on from the carriage or whatever vehicle we can get to carry us there? The least glimpse of his face would satisfy me. That is, to-night."

"I'll try," said Sweetwater, not very sanguine as to the probable result of this effort.

Returning to the stables, he ordered the team. With the last ray of the sun they set out, the reins in Sweetwater's hands.

They headed for the coast-road.

XVIII. THE CLOSED DOOR

The road was once the highway, but the tide having played so many tricks with its numberless bridges a new one had been built farther up the cliff, carrying with it the life and business of the small town. Many old landmarks still remained—shops, warehouses and even a few scattered dwellings. But most of these were deserted, and those that were still in use showed such neglect that it was very evident the whole region would soon be given up to the encroaching sea and such interests as are inseparable from it.

The hour was that mysterious one of late twilight, when outlines lose their distinctness and sea and shore melt into one mass of uniform gray. There was no wind and the waves came in with a soft plash, but so near to the level of the road that it was evident, even to these strangers, that the tide was at its height and would presently begin to ebb.

Soon they had passed the last forsaken dwelling, and the town proper lay behind them. Sand and a few rocks were all that lay between them now and the open stretch of the ocean, which, at this point, approached the land in a small bay, well-guarded on either side by embracing rocky heads. This was what made the harbor at C—.

It was very still. They passed one team and only one. Sweetwater looked very sharply at this team and at its driver, but saw nothing to arouse suspicion. They were now a half-mile from C—, and, seemingly, in a perfectly desolate region.

"A manufactory here!" exclaimed Mr. Grey. It was the first word he had uttered since starting.

"Not far from here," was Sweetwater's equally laconic reply; and, the road taking a turn almost at the moment of his speaking, he leaned forward and pointed out a building standing on the right-hand side of the road, with its feet in the water. "That's it." said he. "They described it well enough for me to know it when I see it. Looks like a robber's hole at this time of night," he laughed; "but what can you expect from a manufactory of patent medicine?"

Mr. Grey was silent. He was looking very earnestly at the building.

"It is larger than I expected," he remarked at last.

Sweetwater himself was surprised, but as they advanced and their point of view changed they found it to be really an insignificant structure, and Mr. Wellgood's portion of it more insignificant still.

In reality it was a collection of three stores under one roof: two of them were shut up and evidently unoccupied, the third showed a lighted window. This was the manufactory. It occupied the middle place and presented a tolerably decent appearance. It showed, besides the lighted lamp I have mentioned, such signs of life as a few packing-boxes tumbled out on the small platform in front, and a whinnying horse attached to an empty buggy, tied to a post on the opposite side of the road.

"I'm glad to see the lamp," muttered Sweetwater. "Now, what shall we do? Is it light enough for you to see his face, if I can manage to bring him to the door?"

Mr. Grey seemed startled.

"It's darker than I thought," said he. "But call the man and if I can not see him plainly, I'll shout to the horse to stand, which you will take as a signal to bring this Wellgood nearer. But do not be surprised if I ride off before he reaches the buggy. I'll come back again and take you up farther down the road."

"All right, sir," answered Sweetwater, with a side glance at the speaker's inscrutable features. "It's a go!" And leaping to the ground he advanced to the manufactory door and knocked loudly.

No one appeared.

He tried the latch; it lifted, but the door did not open; it was fastened from within.

"Strange!" he muttered, casting a glance at the waiting horse and buggy, then at the lighted window, which was on the second floor directly over his head. "Guess I'll sing out."

Here he shouted the man's name. "Wellgood! I say, Wellgood!"

No response to this either.

"Looks bad!" he acknowledged to himself; and, taking a step back, he looked up at the window.

It was closed, but there was neither shade nor curtain to obstruct the view.

"Do you see anything?" he inquired of Mr. Grey, who sat with his eye at the small window in the buggy top.

"Nothing."

"No movement in the room above? No shadow at the window?"

"Nothing."

"Well, it's confounded strange!" And he went back, still calling Wellgood.

The tied-up horse whinnied, and the waves gave a soft splash and that was all,—if I except Sweetwater's muttered oath.

Coming back, he looked again at the window, then, with a gesture toward Mr. Grey, turned the corner of the building and began to edge himself along its side in an endeavor to reach the rear and see what it offered. But he came to a sudden standstill. He found himself on the edge of the bank before he had taken twenty steps. Yet the building projected on, and he saw why it had looked so large from a certain point of the approach. Its rear was built out on piles, making its depth even greater than the united width of the three stores. At low tide this might be accessible from below, but just now the water was almost on a level with the top of the piles, making all approach impossible save by boat.

Disgusted with his failure, Sweetwater returned to the front, and, finding the situation unchanged, took a new resolve. After measuring with his eye the height of the first story, he coolly walked over to the strange horse, and, slipping his bridle, brought it back and cast it over a projection of the door; by its aid he succeeded in climbing up to the window, which was the sole eye to the interior.

Mr. Grey sat far back in his buggy, watching every movement.

There were no shades at the window, as I have before said, and, once Sweetwater's eye had reached the level of the sill, he could see the interior without the least difficulty. There was nobody there. The lamp burned on a great table littered with papers, but the rude cane-chair before it was empty, and so was the room. He could see into every corner of it and there was not even a hiding-place where anybody could remain concealed. Sweetwater was still looking, when the lamp, which had been burning with considerable smoke, flared up and went out. Sweetwater uttered an ejaculation, and, finding himself face to face with utter darkness, slid from his perch to the ground.

Approaching Mr. Grey for the second time, he said:

"I can not understand it. The fellow is either lying low, or he's gone out, leaving his lamp to go out, too. But whose is the horse—just excuse me while I tie him up again. It looks like the one he was driving to-day. It is the one. Well, he won't leave him here all night. Shall we lie low and wait for him to come and unhitch this animal? Or do you prefer to return to the hotel?"

Mr. Grey was slow in answering. Finally he said:

"The man may suspect our intention. You can never tell anything about such fellows as he. He may have caught some unexpected glimpse of me or simply heard that I was in town. If he's the man I think him, he has reasons for avoiding me which I can very well understand. Let us go back,—not to the hotel, I must see this adventure through tonight,—but far enough for him to think we have given up all idea of routing him out to-night. Perhaps that is all he is waiting for. You can steal back—"

"Excuse me," said Sweetwater, "but I know a better dodge than that. We'll circumvent him. We passed a boat-house on our way down here. I'll just drive you up, procure a boat, and bring you back here by water. I don't believe that he will expect that, and if he is in the house we shall see him or his light."

"Meanwhile he can escape by the road."

"Escape? Do you think he is planning to escape?"

The detective spoke with becoming surprise and Mr. Grey answered without apparent suspicion.

"It is possible if he suspects my presence in the neighborhood."

"Do you want to stop him?"

"I want to see him."

"Oh, I remember. Well, sir, we will drive on,—that is, after a moment."

"What are you going to do?"

"Oh, nothing. You said you wanted to see the man before he escaped."

"Yes, but—"

"And that he might escape by the road."

"Yes—"

"Well, I was just making that a little bit impracticable. A small pebble in the keyhole and—why, see now, his horse is walking off! Gee! I must have fastened him badly. I shouldn't wonder if he trotted all the way to town. But it can't be helped. I can not be supposed to race after him. Are you ready now, sir? I'll give another shout, then I'll get in." And once more the lonely region about echoed with the cry: "Wellgood! I say, Wellgood!"

There was no answer, and the young detective, masking for the nonce as Mr. Grey's confidential servant, jumped into the buggy, and turned the horse's head toward C—.

XIX. THE FACE

The moon was well up when the small boat in which our young detective was seated with Mr. Grey appeared in the bay approaching the so-called manufactory of Wellgood. The looked-for light on the waterside was not there. All was dark except where the windows reflected the light of the moon.

This was a decided disappointment to Sweetwater, if not to Mr. Grey. He had expected to detect signs of life in this quarter, and this additional proof of Wellgood's absence from home made it look as if they had come out on a fool's errand and might much better have stuck to the road.

"No promise there," came in a mutter from his lips. "Shall I row in, sir, and try to make a landing?"

"You may row nearer. I should like a closer view. I don't think we shall attract any attention. There are more boats than ours on the water."

Sweetwater was startled. Looking round, he saw a launch, or some such small steamer, riding at anchor not far from the mouth of the bay. But that was not all. Between it and them was a rowboat like their own, resting quietly in the wake of the moon.

"I don't like so much company," he muttered. "Something's brewing; something in which we may not want to take a part."

"Very likely," answered Mr. Grey grimly. "But we must not be deterred— not till I have seen—" the rest Sweetwater did not hear. Mr. Grey seemed to remember himself. "Row nearer," he now bade. "Get under the shadow of the rocks if you can. If the boat is for him, he will show himself. Yet I hardly see how he can board from that bank."

It did not look feasible. Nevertheless, they waited and watched with much patience for several long minutes. The boat behind them did not advance, nor was any movement discernible in the direction of the manufactory. Another short period, then suddenly a light flashed from a window high up in the central gable, sparkled for an instant and was gone. Sweetwater took it for a signal and, with a slight motion of the wrist, began to work his way in toward shore till they lay almost at the edge of the piles.

"Hark!"

It was Sweetwater who spoke.

Both listened, Mr. Grey with his head turned toward the launch and Sweetwater with his eye on the cavernous space, sharply outlined by the piles, which the falling tide now disclosed under each contiguous building. Goods had been directly shipped from these stores in the old days. This he had learned in the village. How shipped he had not been able to understand from his previous survey of the building. But he thought he could see now. At low tide, or better, at half-tide, access could be got to the floor of the extension and, if this floor held a trap, the mystery would be explainable. So would be the hovering boat— the signal-light and—yes! this sound overheard of steps on a rattling planking.

"I hear nothing," whispered Mr. Grey from the other end. "The boat is still there, but not a man has dipped an oar."

"They will soon," returned Sweetwater as a smothered sound of clanking iron reached his ears from the hollow spaces before him. "Duck your head, sir; I'm going to row in under this portion of the house."

Mr. Grey would have protested and with very good reason. There was scarcely a space of three feet between them and the boards overhead. But Sweetwater had so immediately suited action to word that he had no choice.

They were now in utter darkness, and Mr. Grey's thoughts must have been peculiar as he crouched over the stern, hardly knowing what to expect or whether this sudden launch into darkness was for the purpose of flight or pursuit. But enlightenment came soon. The sound of a man's tread in the building above was every moment becoming more perceptible, and while wondering, possibly, at his position, Mr. Grey naturally turned his head as nearly as he could in the direction of these sounds, and was staring with blank eyes into the darkness, when Sweetwater, leaning toward him, whispered:

"Look up! There's a trap. In a minute he'll open it. Mark him, but don't breathe a word, and I'll get you out of this all right."

Mr. Grey attempted some answer, but it was lost in the prolonged creak of slowly-moving hinges somewhere over their heads. Spaces, which had looked dark, suddenly looked darker; hearing was satisfied, but not the eye. A man's breath panting with exertion testified to a near-by presence; but that man was working without a light in a room with shuttered windows, and Mr. Grey probably felt that he knew very little more than before, when suddenly, most unexpectedly, to him at least, a face started out of that overhead darkness; a face so white, with every feature made so startlingly distinct by the strong light Sweetwater had thrown upon it, that it seemed the only thing in the world to the two men beneath. In another moment it had vanished, or rather the light which had revealed it.

"What's that? Are you there?" came down from above in hoarse and none too encouraging tones.

There was none to answer; Sweetwater, with a quick pull on the oars, had already shot the boat out of its dangerous harbor.

XX. MOONLIGHT—AND A CLUE

"Are you satisfied? Have you got what you wanted?" asked Sweetwater, when they were well away from the shore and the voice they had heard calling at intervals from the chasm they had left.

"Yes. You're a good fellow. It could not have been better managed." Then, after a pause too prolonged and thoughtful to please Sweetwater, who was burning with curiosity if not with some deeper feeling: "What was that light you burned? A match?"

Sweetwater did not answer. He dared not. How speak of the electric torch he as a detective carried in his pocket? That would be to give himself away. He therefore let this question slip by and put in one of his own.

"Are you ready to go back now, sir? Are we all done here?" This with his ear turned and his eye bent forward; for the adventure they had interrupted was not at an end, whether their part in it was or not.

Mr. Grey hesitated, his glances following those of Sweetwater.

"Let us wait," said he, in a tone which surprised Sweetwater. "If he is meditating an escape, I must speak to him before he reaches the launch. At all hazards," he added after another moment's thought.

"All right, sir—How do you propose—"

His words were interrupted by a shrill whistle from the direction of the bank. Promptly, and as if awaiting this signal, the two men in the rowboat before them dipped their oars and pulled for the shore, taking the direction of the manufactory.

Sweetwater said nothing, but held himself in readiness.

Mr. Grey was equally silent, but the lines of his face seemed to deepen in the moonlight as the boat, gliding rapidly through the water, passed them within a dozen boat-lengths and slipped into the opening under the manufactory building.

"Now row!" he cried. "Make for the launch. We'll intercept them on their return."

Sweetwater, glowing with anticipation, bent to his work. The boat beneath them gave a bound and in a few minutes they were far out on the waters of the bay.

"They're coming!" he whispered eagerly, as he saw Mr. Grey looking anxiously back. "How much farther shall I go?"

"Just within hailing distance of the launch," was Mr. Grey's reply.

Sweetwater, gauging the distance with a glance, stopped at the proper point and rested on his oars. But his thoughts did not rest. He realized that he was about to witness an interview whose importance he easily recognized. How much of it would he hear? What would be the upshot and what was his full duty in the case? He knew that this man Wellgood was wanted by the New York police, but he was possessed with no authority to arrest him, even if he had the power.

"Something more than I bargained for," he inwardly commented. "But I wanted excitement, and now I have got it. If only I can keep my head level, I may get something out of this, if not all I could wish."

Meantime the second boat was very nearly on them. He could mark the three figures and pick out Wellgood's head from among the rest. It had a resolute air; the face on which, to his evident discomfiture, the moon shone, wore a look which convinced the detective that this was no patent-medicine manufacturer, nor even a caterer's assistant, but a man of nerve and resources, the same, indeed, whom he had encountered in Mr. Fairbrother's house, with such disastrous, almost fatal, results to himself.

The discovery, though an unexpected one, did not lessen his sense of the extreme helplessness of his own position. He could witness, but he could not act; follow Mr. Grey's orders, but indulge in none of his own. The detective must continue to be lost in the valet, though it came hard and woke a sense of shame in his ambitious breast.

Meanwhile Wellgood had seen them and ordered his men to cease rowing.

"Give way, there," he shouted. "We're for the launch and in a hurry."

"There's some one here who wants to speak to you, Mr. Wellgood," Sweetwater called out, as respectfully as he could. "Shall I mention your name?" he asked of Mr. Grey.

"No, I will do that myself." And raising his voice, he accosted the other with these words: "I am the man, Percival Grey, of Darlington Manor, England. I should like to say a word to you before you embark."

A change, quick as lightning and almost as dangerous, passed over the face Sweetwater was watching with such painful anxiety; but as the other added nothing to his words and seemed to be merely waiting, he shrugged his shoulders and muttered an order to his rowers to proceed.

In another moment the sterns of the two small craft swung together, but in such a way that, by dint of a little skilful manipulation on the part of Wellgood's men, the latter's back was toward the moon.

Mr. Grey leaned toward Wellgood, and his face fell into shadow also.

"Bah!" thought the detective, "I should have managed that myself. But if I can not see I shall at least hear."

But he deceived himself in this. The two men spoke in such low whispers that only their intensity was manifest. Not a word came to Sweetwater's ears.

"Bah!" he thought again, "this is bad."

But he had to swallow his disappointment, and more. For presently the two men, so different in culture, station and appearance, came, as it seemed, to an understanding, and Wellgood, taking his hand from his breast, fumbled in one of his pockets and drew out something which he handed to Mr. Grey.

This made Sweetwater start and peer with still greater anxiety at every movement, when to his surprise both bent forward, each over his own knee, doing something so mysterious he could get no clue to its nature till they again stretched forth their hands to each other and he caught the gleam of paper and realized that they were exchanging memoranda or notes.

These must have been important, for each made an immediate endeavor to read his slip by turning it toward the moon's rays. That both were satisfied was shown by their after movements. Wellgood put his slip into his pocket, and without further word to Mr. Grey motioned his men to row away. They did so with a will, leaving a line of silver in their wake. Mr. Grey, on the contrary, gave no orders. He still held his slip and seemed to be dreaming. But his eye was on the shore, and he did not even turn when sounds from the launch denoted that she was under way.

Sweetwater; looking at this morsel of paper with greedy eyes, dipped his oars and began pulling softly toward that portion of the beach where a small and twinkling light defined the boat-house. He hoped Mr. Grey would speak, hoped that in some way, by some means, he might obtain a clue to his patron's thoughts. But the English gentleman sat like an image and did not move till a slight but sudden breeze, blowing in-shore, seized the paper in his hand and carried it away, past Sweetwater, who vainly sought to catch it as it went fluttering by, into the water ahead, where it shone for a moment, then softly disappeared.

Sweetwater uttered a cry, so did Mr. Grey.

"Is it anything you wanted?" called out the former, leaning over the bow of the boat and making a dive at the paper with his oar.

"Yes; but if it's gone, it's gone," returned the other with some feeling. "Careless of me, very careless,—but I was thinking of—"

He stopped; he was greatly agitated, but he did not encourage Sweetwater in any further attempts to recover the lost memorandum. Indeed, such an effort would have been fruitless; the paper was gone, and there was nothing left for them but to continue their way. As they did so it would have been hard to tell in which breast chagrin mounted higher. Sweetwater had lost a clue in a thousand, and Mr. Greywell, no one knew what he had lost. He said nothing and plainly showed by his changed manner that he was in haste to land now and be done with this doubtful adventure.

When they reached the boat-house Mr. Grey left Sweetwater to pay for the boat and started at once for the hotel.

The man in charge had the bow of the boat in hand, preparatory to pulling it up on the boards. As Sweetwater turned toward him he caught sight of the side of the boat, shining brightly in the moonlight. He gave a start and, with a muttered ejaculation, darted forward and picked off a small piece of paper from the dripping keel. It separated in his hand and a part of it escaped him, but the rest he managed to keep by secreting it in his palm, where it still clung, wet and possibly illegible, when he came upon Mr. Grey again in the hotel office.

"Here's your pay," said that gentleman, giving him a bill. "I am very glad I met you. You have served me remarkably well."

There was an anxiety in his face and a hurry in his movements which struck Sweetwater.

"Does this mean that you are through with me?" asked Sweetwater. "That you have no further call for my services?"

"Quite so," said the gentleman. "I'm going to take the train to-night. I find that I still have time."

Sweetwater began to look alive.

Uttering hasty thanks, he rushed away to his own room and, turning on the gas, peeled off the morsel of paper which had begun to dry on his hand. If it should prove to be the blank end! If the written part were the one which had floated off! Such disappointments had fallen to his lot! He was not unused to them.

But he was destined to better luck this time. The written end had indeed disappeared, but there was one word left, which he had no sooner read than he gave a low cry and prepared to leave for New York on the same train as Mr. Grey.

The word was—diamond.

XXI. GRIZEL! GRIZEL!

I indulged in some very serious thoughts after Mr. Grey's departure. A fact was borne in upon me to which I had hitherto closed my prejudiced eyes, but which I could no longer ignore, whatever confusion it brought or however it caused me to change my mind on a subject which had formed one of the strongest bases to the argument by which I had sought to save Mr. Durand. Miss Grey cherished no such distrust of her father as I, in my ignorance of their relations, had imputed to her in the early hours of my ministrations. This you have already seen in my account of their parting. Whatever his dread, fear or remorse, there was no evidence that she felt toward him anything but love and confidence: but love and confidence from her to him were in direct contradiction to the doubts I had believed her to have expressed in the half-written note handed to Mrs. Fairbrother in the alcove. Had I been wrong, then, in attributing this scrawl to her? It began to look so. Though forbidden to allow her to speak on the one tabooed subject, I had wit enough to know that nothing would keep her from it, if the fate of Mrs. Fairbrother occupied any real place in her thoughts.

Yet when the opportunity was given me one morning of settling this fact beyond all doubt, I own that my main feeling was one of dread. I feared to see this article in my creed destroyed, lest I should lose confidence in the whole. Yet conscience bade me face the matter boldly, for had I not boasted to myself that my one desire was the truth?

I allude to the disposition which Miss Grey showed on the morning of the third day to do a little surreptitious writing. You remember that a specimen of her handwriting had been asked for by the inspector, and once had been earnestly desired by myself. Now I seemed likely to have it, if I did not open my eyes too widely to the meaning of her seemingly chance requests. A little pencil dangled at the end of my watch-chain. Would I let her see it, let her hold it in her hand for a minute? it was so like one she used to have. Of course I took it off, of course I let her retain it a little while in her hand. But the pencil was not enough. A few minutes later she asked for a book to look at—I sometimes let her look at pictures. But the book bothered her—she would look at it later; would I give her something to mark the place—that postal over there. I gave her the postal. She put it in the book and I, who understood her thoroughly, wondered what excuse she would now find for sending me into the other room. She found one very soon, and with a heavily-beating heart I left her with that pencil and postal. A soft laugh from her lips drew me back. She was holding up the postal.

"See! I have written a line to him! Oh, you good, good nurse, to let me! You needn't look so alarmed. It hasn't hurt me one bit."

I knew that it had not; knew that such an exertion was likely to be more beneficial than hurtful to her, or I should have found some excuse for deterring her. I endeavored to make my face more natural. As she seemed to want me to take the postal in my hand I drew near and took it.

"The address looks very shaky," she laughed. "I think you will have to put it in an envelope."

I looked at it,—I could not help it,—her eye was on me, and I could not even prepare my mind for the shock of seeing it like or totally unlike the writing of the warning. It was totally unlike; so distinctly unlike that it was no longer possible to attribute those lines to her which, according to Mr. Durand's story, had caused Mrs. Fairbrother to take off her diamond.

"Why, why!" she cried. "You actually look pale. Are you afraid the doctor will scold us? It hasn't hurt me nearly so much as lying here and knowing what he would give for one word from me."

"You are right, and I am foolish," I answered with all the spirit left in me. "I should be glad—I am glad that you have written these words. I will copy the address on an envelope and send it out in the first mail."

"Thank you," she murmured, giving me back my pencil with a sly smile. "Now I can sleep. I must have roses in my cheeks when papa comes home."

And she bade fair to have ruddier roses than myself, for conscience was working havoc in my breast. The theory I had built up with such care, the theory I had persisted in urging upon the inspector in spite of his rebuke, was slowly crumbling to pieces in my mind with the falling of one of its main pillars. With the warning unaccounted for in the manner I have stated, there was a weakness in my argument which nothing could make good. How could I tell the inspector, if ever I should be so happy or so miserable as to meet his eye again? Humiliated to the dust, I could see no worth now in any of the arguments I had advanced. I flew from one extreme to the other, and was imputing perfect probity to Mr. Grey and an honorable if mysterious reason for all his acts, when the door opened and he came in. Instantly my last doubt vanished. I had not expected him to return so soon.

He was glad to be back; that I could see, but there was no other gladness in him. I had looked for some change in his manner and appearance,—that is, if he returned at all,—but the one I saw was not a cheerful one, even after he had approached his daughter's bedside and found her greatly improved. She noticed this and scrutinized him strangely. He dropped his eyes and turned to leave the room, but was stopped by her loving cry; he came back and leaned over her.

"What is it, father? You are fatigued, worried—"

"No, no, quite well," he hastily assured her. "But you! are you as well as you seem?"

"Indeed, yes. I am gaining every day. See! see! I shall soon be able to sit up. Yesterday I read a few words."

He started, with a side glance at me which took in a table near by on which a little book was lying.

"Oh, a book?"

"Yes, and—and Arthur's letters."

The father flushed, lifted himself, patted her arm tenderly and hastened into another room.

Miss Grey's eyes followed him longingly, and I heard her give utterance to a soft sigh. A few hours before, this would have conveyed to my suspicious mind deep and mysterious meanings; but I was seeing everything now in a different light, and I found myself no longer inclined either to exaggerate or to misinterpret these little marks of filial solicitude. Trying to rejoice over the present condition of my mind, I was searching in the hidden depths of my nature for the patience of which I stood in such need, when every thought and feeling were again thrown into confusion by the receipt of another communication from the inspector, in which he stated that something had occurred to bring the authorities round to my way of thinking and that the test with the stiletto was to be made at once.

Could the irony of fate go further! I dropped the letter half read, querying if it were my duty to let the inspector know of the flaw I had discovered in my own theory, before I proceeded with the attempt I had suggested when I believed in its complete soundness. I had not settled the question when I took the letter up again. Re-reading its opening sentence, I was caught by the word "something." It was a very indefinite one, yet was capable of covering a large field. It must cover a large field, or it could not have produced such a change in the minds of these men, conservative from principle and in this instance from discretion. I would be satisfied with that word something and quit further thinking. I was weary of it. The inspector was now taking the initiative, and I was satisfied to be his simple instrument and no more. Arrived at this conclusion, however, I read the rest of the letter. The test was to go on, but under different conditions. It was no longer to be made at my own discretion and in the up-stairs room; it was to be made at luncheon hour and in Mr. Grey's private dining-room, where, if by any chance Mr. Grey found himself outraged by the placing of this notorious weapon beside his plate, the blame could be laid on the waiter, who, mistaking his directions, had placed it on Mr. Grey's table when it was meant for Inspector Dalzell's, who was lunching in the adjoining room. It was I, however, who was to do the placing. With what precautions and under what circumstances will presently appear.

Fortunately, the hour set was very near. Otherwise I do not know how I could have endured the continued strain of gazing on my patient's sweet face, looking up at me from her pillow, with a shadow over its beauty which had not been there before her father's return.

And that father! I could hear him pacing the library floor with a restlessness that struck me as being strangely akin to my own inward anguish of impatience and doubt. What was he dreading? What was it I had seen darkening his face and disturbing his manner, when from time to time he pushed open the communicating door and cast an anxious glance our way, only to withdraw again without uttering a word. Did he realize that a crisis was approaching, that danger menaced him, and from me? No, not the latter, for his glance never strayed to me, but rested solely on his daughter. I was, therefore, not connected with the disturbance in his thoughts. As far as that was concerned I could proceed fearlessly; I had not him to dread, only the event. That I did dread, as any one must who saw Miss Grey's face during these painful moments and heard that restless tramp in the room beyond.

At last the hour struck,—the hour at which Mr. Grey always descended to lunch. He was punctuality itself, and under ordinary circumstances I could depend upon his leaving the room within five minutes of the stroke of one. But would he be as prompt to-day? Was he in the mood for luncheon? Would he go down stairs at all? Yes, for the tramp, tramp stopped; I heard him approaching his daughter's door for a last look in and managed to escape just in time to procure what I wanted and reach the room below before he came.

My opportunity was short, but I had time to see two things: first, that the location of his seat had been changed so that his back was to the door leading into the adjoining room; secondly, that this door was ajar. The usual waiter was in the room and showed no surprise at my appearance, I having been careful to have it understood that hereafter Miss Grey's appetite was to be encouraged by having her soup served from her father's table by her father's own hands, and that I should be there to receive it.

"Mr. Grey is coming," said I, approaching the waiter and handing him the stiletto loosely wrapped in tissue paper. "Will you be kind enough to place this at his plate, just as it is? A man gave it to me for Mr. Grey; said we were to place it there."

The waiter, suspecting nothing, did as he was bidden, and I had hardly time to catch up the tray laden with dishes, which I saw awaiting me on a side-table, when Mr. Grey came in and was ushered to his seat.

The soup was not there, but I advanced with my tray and stood waiting; not too near, lest the violent beating of my heart should betray me. As I did so the waiter disappeared and the door behind us opened. Though Mr. Grey's eye had fallen on the package, and I saw him start, I darted one glance at the room thus disclosed, and saw that it held two tables. At one, the inspector and some one I did not know sat eating; at the other a man alone, whose back was to us all, and who seemingly was entirely disconnected with the interests of this tragic moment. All this I saw in an instant,—the next my eyes were fixed on Mr. Grey's face.

He had reached out his hand to the package and his features showed an emotion I hardly understood.

"What's this?" he murmured, feeling it with wonder, I should almost say anger. Suddenly he pulled off the wrapper, and my heart stood still in expectancy. If he quailed—and how could he help doing so if guilty—what a doubt would be removed from my own breast, what an impediment from police action! But he did not quail; he simply uttered an exclamation of intense anger, and laid the weapon back on the table without even taking the precaution of covering it up. I think he muttered an oath, but there was no fear in it, not a particle.

My disappointment was so great, my humiliation so unbounded, that, forgetting myself in my dismay, I staggered back and let the tray with all its contents slip from my hands. The crash that followed stopped Mr. Grey in the act of rising. But it did something more. It awoke a cry from the adjoining room which I shall never forget. While we both started and turned to see from whom this grievous sound had sprung, a man came stumbling toward us with his hands before his eyes and this name wild on his lips:

"Grizel! Grizel!"

Mrs. Fairbrother's name! and the man—

XXII. GUILT

Was he Wellgood? Sears? Who? A lover of the woman certainly; that was borne in on us by the passion of his cry:

"Grizel! Grizel!"

But how here? and why such fury in Mr. Grey's face and such amazement in that of the inspector?

This question was not to be answered offhand. Mr. Grey, advancing, laid a finger on the man's shoulder. "Come," said he, "we will have our conversation in another room."

The man, who, in dress and appearance looked oddly out of place in those gorgeous rooms, shook off the stupor into which he had fallen and started to follow the Englishman. A waiter crossed their track with the soup for our table. Mr. Grey motioned him aside.

"Take that back," said he. "I have some business to transact with this gentleman before I eat. I'll ring when I want you."

Then they entered where I was. As the door closed I caught sight of the inspector's face turned earnestly toward me. In his eyes I read my duty, and girded up my heart, as it were, to meet—what? In that moment it was impossible to tell.

The next enlightened me. With a total ignoring of my presence, due probably to his great excitement, Mr. Grey turned on his companion the moment he had closed the door and, seizing him by the collar, cried:

"Fairbrother, you villain, why have you called on your wife like this? Are you murderer as well as thief?"

Fairbrother! this man? Then who was he who was being nursed back to life on the mountains beyond Santa Fe? Sears? Anything seemed possible in that moment.

Meanwhile, dropping his hand from the other's throat as suddenly as he had seized it, Mr. Grey caught up the stiletto from the table where he had flung it, crying: "Do you recognize this?"

Ah, then I saw guilt!

In a silence worse than any cry, this so-called husband of the murdered woman, the man on whom no suspicion had fallen, the man whom all had thought a thousand miles away at the time of the deed, stared at the weapon thrust under his eyes, while over his face passed all those expressions of fear, abhorrence and detected guilt which, fool that I was, I had expected to see reflected in response to the same test in Mr. Grey's equable countenance.

The surprise and wonder of it held me chained to the spot. I was in a state of stupefaction, so that I scarcely noted the broken fragments at my feet. But the intruder noticed them. Wrenching his gaze from the stiletto which Mr. Grey continued to hold out, he pointed to the broken cup and saucer, muttering:

"That is what startled me into this betrayal—the noise of breaking china. I can not bear it since—"

He stopped, bit his lip and looked around him with an air of sudden bravado.

"Since you dropped the cups at your wife's feet in Mr. Ramsdell's alcove," finished Mr. Grey with admirable self-possession.

"I see that explanations from myself are not in order," was the grim retort, launched with the bitterest sarcasm. Then as the full weight of his position crushed in on him, his face assumed an aspect startling to my unaccustomed eyes, and, thrusting his hand into his pocket he drew forth a small box which he placed in Mr. Grey's hands.

"The Great Mogul," he declared simply.

It was the first time I had heard this diamond so named.

Without a word that gentleman opened the box, took one look at the contents, assumed a satisfied air, and carefully deposited the recovered gem in his own pocket. As his eyes returned to the man before him, all the passion of the latter burst forth.

"It was not for that I killed her!" cried he. "It was because she defied me and flaunted her disobedience in my very face. I would do it again, yet—"

Here his voice broke and it was in a different tone and with a total change of manner he added: "You stand appalled at my depravity. You have not lived my life." Then quickly and with a touch of sullenness: "You suspected me because of the stiletto. It was a mistake, using that stiletto. Otherwise, the plan was good. I doubt if you know now how I found my way into the alcove, possibly under your very eyes; certainly, under the eyes of many who knew me."

"I do not. It is enough that you entered it; that you confess your guilt."

Here Mr. Grey stretched his hand toward the electric button.

"No, it is not enough." The tone was fierce, authoritative. "Do not ring the bell, not yet. I have a fancy to tell you how I managed that little affair."

Glancing about, he caught up from a near-by table a small brass tray. Emptying it of its contents, he turned on us with drawn-down features and an obsequious air so opposed to his natural manner that it was as if another man stood before us.

"Pardon my black tie," he muttered, holding out the tray toward Mr. Grey.

Wellgood!

The room turned with me. It was he, then, the great financier, the multimillionaire, the husband of the magnificent Grizel, who had entered Mr. Ramsdell's house as a waiter!

Mr. Grey did not show surprise, but he made a gesture, when instantly the tray was thrown aside and the man resumed his ordinary aspect.

"I see you understand me," he cried. "I who have played host at many a ball, passed myself off that night as one of the waiters. I came and went and no one noticed me. It is such a natural sight to see a waiter passing ices that my going in and out of the alcove did not attract the least attention. I never look at waiters when I attend balls. I never look higher than their trays. No one looked at me higher than my tray. I held the stiletto under the tray and when I struck her she threw up her hands and they hit the tray and the cups fell. I have never been able to bear the sound of breaking china since. I loved her—"

A gasp and he recovered himself.

"That is neither here nor there," he muttered. "You summoned me under threat to present myself at your door to-day. I have done so. I meant to restore you your diamond, simply. It has become worthless to me. But fate exacted more. Surprise forced my secret from me. That young lady with her damnable awkwardness has put my head in a noose. But do not think to hold it there. I did not risk this interview without precautions, I assure you, and when I leave this hotel it will be as a free man."

With one of his rapid changes, wonderful and inexplicable to me at the moment, he turned toward me with a bow, saying courteously enough:

"We will excuse the young lady."

Next moment the barrel of a pistol gleamed in his hand.

The moment was critical. Mr. Grey stood directly in the line of fire, and the audacious man who thus held him at his mercy was scarcely a foot from the door leading into the hall. Marking the desperation of his look and the steadiness of his finger on the trigger, I expected to see Mr. Grey recoil and the man escape. But Mr. Grey held his own, though he made no move, and did not venture to speak. Nerved by his courage, I summoned up all my own. This man must not escape, nor must Mr. Grey suffer. The pistol directed against him must be diverted to myself. Such amends were due one whose good name I had so deeply if secretly insulted. I had but to scream, to call out for the inspector, but a remembrance of the necessity we were now under of preserving our secret, of keeping from Mr. Grey the fact that he had been under surveillance, was even at that moment surrounded by the police, deterred me, and I threw myself toward the bell instead, crying out that I would raise the house if he moved, and laid my finger on the button.

The pistol swerved my way. The face above it smiled. I watched that smile. Before it broadened to its full extent, I pressed the button.

Fairbrother stared, dropped his pistol, and burst forth with these two words:

"Brave girl!"

The tone I can never convey.

Then he made for the door.

As he laid his hand on the knob, he called back:

"I have been in worse straits than this!"

But he never had; when he opened the door, he found himself face to face with the inspector.

XXIII. THE GREAT MOGUL

Later, it was all explained. Mr. Grey, looking like another man, came into the room where I was endeavoring to soothe his startled daughter and devour in secret my own joy. Taking the sweet girl in his arms, he said, with a calm ignoring of my presence, at which I secretly smiled:

"This is the happiest moment of my existence, Helen. I feel as if I had recovered you from the brink of the grave."

"Me? Why, I have never been so ill as that."

"I know; but I have felt as if you were doomed ever since I heard, or thought I heard, in this city, and under no ordinary circumstances, the peculiar cry which haunts our house on the eve of any great misfortune. I shall not apologize for my fears; you know that I have good cause for them, but to-day, only to-day, I have heard from the lips of the most arrant knave I have ever known, that this cry sprang from himself with intent to deceive me. He knew my weakness; knew the cry; he was in Darlington Manor when Cecilia died; and, wishing to startle me into dropping something which I held, made use of his ventriloquial powers (he had been a mountebank once, poor wretch!) and with such effect, that I have not been a happy man since, in spite of your daily improvement and continued promise of recovery. But I am happy now, relieved and joyful; and this miserable being,—would you like to hear his story? Are you strong enough for anything so tragic? He is a thief and a murderer, but he has feelings, and his life has been a curious one, and strangely interwoven with ours. Do you care to hear about it? He is the man who stole our diamond."

My patient uttered a little cry.

"Oh, tell me," she entreated, excited, but not unhealthfully; while I was in an anguish of curiosity I could with difficulty conceal.

Mr. Grey turned with courtesy toward me and asked if a few family details would bore me. I smiled and assured him to the contrary. At which he settled himself in the chair he liked best and began a tale which I will permit myself to present to you complete and from other points of view than his own.

Some five years before, one of the great diamonds of the world was offered for sale in an Eastern market. Mr. Grey, who stopped at no expense in the gratification of his taste in this direction, immediately sent his agent to Egypt to examine this stone. If the agent discovered it to be all that was claimed for it, and within the reach of a wealthy commoner's purse, he was to buy it. Upon inspection, it was found to be all that was claimed, with one exception. In the center of one of the facets was a flaw, but, as this was considered to mark the diamond, and rather add to than detract from its value as a traditional stone with many historical associations, it was finally purchased by Mr. Grey and placed among his treasures in his manor-house in Kent. Never a suspicious man, he took delight in exhibiting this acquisition to such of his friends and acquaintances as were likely to feel any interest in it, and it was not an uncommon thing for him to allow it to pass from hand to hand while he pottered over his other treasures and displayed this and that to such as had no eyes for the diamond.

It was after one such occasion that he found, on taking the stone in his hand to replace it in the safe he had had built for it in one of his cabinets, that it did not strike his eye with its usual force and brilliancy, and, on examining it closely, he discovered the absence of the telltale flaw. Struck with dismay, he submitted it to a still more rigid inspection, when he found that what he held was not even a diamond, but a worthless bit of glass, which had been substituted by some cunning knave for his invaluable gem.

For the moment his humiliation almost equaled his sense of loss; he had been so often warned of the danger he ran in letting so priceless an object pass around under all eyes but his own. His wife and friends had prophesied some such loss as this, not once, but many times, and he had always laughed at their fears, saying that he knew his friends, and there was not a scamp amongst them. But now he saw it proved that even the intuition of a man well-versed in human nature is not always infallible, and, ashamed of his past laxness and more ashamed yet of the doubts which this experience called up in regard to all his friends, he shut up the false stone with his usual care and buried his loss in his own bosom, till he could sift his impressions and recall with some degree of probability the circumstances under which this exchange could have been made.

It had not been made that evening. Of this he was positive. The only persons present on this occasion were friends of such standing and repute that suspicion in their regard was simply monstrous. When and to whom, then, had he shown the diamond last? Alas, it had been a long month since he had shown the jewel. Cecilia, his youngest daughter, had died in the interim; therefore his mind had not been on jewels. A month! time for his precious diamond to have been carried back to the East! Time for it to have been recut! Surely it was lost to him for ever, unless he could immediately locate the person who had robbed him of it.

But this promised difficulties. He could not remember just what persons he had entertained on that especial day in his little hall of cabinets, and, when he did succeed in getting a list of them from his butler, he was by no means sure that it included the full number of his guests. His own memory was execrable, and, in short, he had but few facts to offer to the discreet agent sent up from Scotland Yard one morning to hear his complaint and act secretly in his interests. He could give him carte blanche to carry on his inquiries in the diamond market, but little else. And while this seemed to satisfy the agent, it did not lead to any gratifying result to himself, and he had thoroughly made up his mind to swallow his loss and say nothing about it, when one day a young cousin of his, living in great style in an adjoining county, informed him that in some mysterious way he had lost from his collection of arms a unique and highly-prized stiletto of Italian workmanship.

Startled by this coincidence, Mr. Grey ventured upon a question or two, which led to his cousin's confiding to him the fact that this article had disappeared after a large supper given by him to a number of friends and gentlemen from London. This piece of knowledge, still further coinciding with his own experience, caused Mr. Grey to ask for a list of his guests, in the hope of finding among them one who had been in his own house.

His cousin, quite unsuspicious of the motives underlying this request, hastened to write out this list, and together they pored over the names, crossing out such as were absolutely above suspicion. When they had reached the end of the list, but two names remained uncrossed. One was that of a rattle-pated youth who had come in the wake of a highly reputed connection of theirs, and the other that of an American tourist who gave all the evidences of great wealth and had presented letters to leading men in London which had insured him attentions not usually accorded to foreigners. This man's name was Fairbrother, and, the moment Mr. Grey heard it, he recalled the fact that an American with a peculiar name, but with a reputation for wealth, had been among his guests on the suspected evening.

Hiding the effect produced upon him by this discovery, he placed his finger on this name and begged his cousin to look up its owner's antecedents and present reputation in America; but, not content with this, he sent his own agent over to New York—whither, as he soon learned, this gentleman had returned. The result was an apparent vindication of the suspected American. He was found to be a well-known citizen of the great metropolis, moving in the highest circles and with a reputation for wealth won by an extraordinary business instinct.

To be sure, he had not always enjoyed these distinctions. Like many another self-made man, he had risen from a menial position in a Western mining camp, to be the owner of a mine himself, and so up through the various gradations of a successful life to a position among the foremost business men of New York. In all these changes he had maintained a name for honest, if not generous, dealing. He lived in great style, had married and was known to have but one extravagant fancy. This was for the unique and curious in art,—a taste which, if report spoke true, cost him many thousands each year.

This last was the only clause in the report which pointed in any way toward this man being the possible abstractor of the Great Mogul, as Mr. Grey's famous diamond was called, and the latter was too just a man and too much of a fancier in this line himself to let a fact of this kind weigh against the favorable nature of the rest. So he recalled his agent, double-locked his cabinets and continued to confine his display of valuables to articles which did not suggest jewels. Thus three years passed, when one day he heard mention made of a wonderful diamond which had been seen in New York. From its description he gathered that it must be the one surreptitiously abstracted from his cabinet, and when, after some careful inquiries, he learned that the name of its possessor was Fairbrother, he awoke to his old suspicions and determined to probe this matter to the bottom. But secretly. He still had too much consideration to attack a man in high position without full proof.

Knowing of no one he could trust with so delicate an inquiry as this had now become, he decided to undertake it himself, and for this purpose embraced the first opportunity to cross the water. He took his daughter with him because he had resolved never to let his one remaining child out of his sight. But she knew nothing of his plans or reason for travel. No one did. Indeed, only his lawyer and the police were aware of the loss of his diamond.

His first surprise on landing was to learn that Mr. Fairbrother, of whose marriage he had heard, had quarreled with his wife and that, in the separation which had occurred, the diamond had fallen to her share and was consequently in her possession at the present moment.

This changed matters, and Mr. Grey's only thought now was to surprise her with the diamond on her person and by one glance assure himself that it was indeed the Great Mogul. Since Mrs. Fairbrother was reported to be a beautiful woman and a great society belle, he saw no reason why he should not meet her publicly, and that very soon. He therefore accepted invitations and attended theaters and balls, though his daughter had suffered from her voyage and was not able to accompany him. But alas! he soon learned that Mrs. Fairbrother was never seen with her diamond and, one evening after an introduction at the opera, that she never talked about it. So there he was, balked on the very threshold of his enterprise, and, recognizing the fact, was preparing to take his now seriously ailing daughter south, when he received an invitation to a ball of such a select character that he decided to remain for it, in the hope that Mrs. Fairbrother would be tempted to put on all her splendor for so magnificent a function and thus gratify him with a sight of his own diamond. During the days that intervened he saw her several times and very soon decided that, in spite of her reticence in regard to this gem, she was not sufficiently in her husband's confidence to know the secret of its real ownership. This encouraged him to attempt piquing her into wearing the diamond on this occasion. He talked of precious stones and finally of his own, declaring that he had a connoisseur's eye for a fine diamond, but had seen none as yet in America to compete with a specimen or two he had in his own cabinets. Her eye flashed at this and, though she said nothing, he felt sure that her presence at Mr. Ramsdell's house would be enlivened by her great jewel.

So much for Mr. Grey's attitude in this matter up to the night of the ball. It is interesting enough, but that of Abner Fairbrother is more interesting still and much more serious.

His was indeed the hand which had abstracted the diamond from Mr. Grey's collection. Under ordinary conditions he was an honest man. He prized his good name and would not willingly risk it, but he had little real conscience, and once his passions were aroused nothing short of the object desired would content him. At once forceful and subtle, he had at his command infinite resources which his wandering and eventful life had heightened almost to the point of genius. He saw this stone, and at once felt an inordinate desire to possess it. He had coveted other men's treasures before, but not as he coveted this. What had been longing in other cases was mania in this. There was a woman in America whom he loved. She was beautiful and she was splendor-loving. To see her with this glory on her breast would be worth almost any risk which his imagination could picture at the moment. Before the diamond had left his hand he had made up his mind to have it for his own. He knew that it could not be bought, so he set about obtaining it by an act he did not hesitate to acknowledge to himself as criminal. But he did not act without precautions. Having a keen eye and a proper sense or size and color, he carried away from his first view of it a true image of the stone, and when he was next admitted to Mr. Grey's cabinet room he had provided the means for deceiving the owner whose character he had sounded.

He might have failed in his daring attempt if he had not been favored by a circumstance no one could have foreseen. A daughter of the house, Cecilia by name, lay critically ill at the time, and Mr. Grey's attention was more or less distracted. Still the probabilities are that he would have noticed something amiss with the stone when he came to restore it to its place, if, just as he took it in his hand, there had not risen in the air outside a weird and wailing cry which at once seized upon the imagination of the dozen gentlemen present, and so nearly prostrated their host that he thrust the box he held unopened into the safe and fell upon his knees, a totally unnerved man, crying:

"The banshee! the banshee! My daughter will die!"

Another hand than his locked the safe and dropped the key into the distracted father's pocket.

Thus a superhuman daring conjoined with a special intervention of fate had made the enterprise a successful one; and Fairbrother, believing more than ever in his star, carried this invaluable jewel back with him to New York. The stiletto—well, the taking of that was a folly, for which he had never ceased to blush. He had not stolen it; he would not steal so inconsiderable an object. He had merely put it in his pocket when he saw it forgotten, passed over, given to him, as it were. That the risk, contrary to that involved in the taking of the diamond, was far in excess of the gratification obtained, he realized almost immediately, but, having made the break, and acquired the curio, he spared himself all further thought or the consequences, and presently resumed his old life in New York, none the worse, to all appearances, for these escapades from virtue and his usual course of fair and open dealing.

But he was soon the worse from jealousy of the wife which his new possession had possibly won for him. She had answered all his expectations as mistress of his home and the exponent of his wealth; and for a year, nay, for two, he had been perfectly happy. Indeed, he had been more than that; he had been triumphant, especially on that memorable evening when, after a cautious delay of months, he had dared to pin that unapproachable sparkler to her breast and present her thus bedecked to the smart set—her whom his talents, and especially his far-reaching business talents, had made his own.

Recalling the old days of barter and sale across the pine counter in Colorado, he felt that his star rode high, and for a time was satisfied with his wife's magnificence and the prestige she gave his establishment. But pride is not all, even to a man of his daring ambition. Gradually he began to realize, first, that she was indifferent to him, next, that she despised him, and, lastly, that she hated him. She had dozens at her feet, any of whom was more agreeable to her than her own husband; and, though he could not put his finger on any definite fault, he soon wearied of a beauty that only glowed for others, and made up his mind to part with her rather than let his heart be eaten out by unappeasable longing for what his own good sense told him would never be his.

Yet, being naturally generous, he was satisfied with a separation, and, finding it impossible to think of her as other than extravagantly fed, waited on and clothed, he allowed her a good share of his fortune with the one proviso, that she should not disgrace him. But the diamond she stole, or rather carried off in her naturally high-handed manner with the rest of her jewels. He had never given it to her. She knew the value he set on it, but not how he came by it, and would have worn it quite freely if he had not very soon given her to understand that the pleasure of doing so ceased when she left his house. As she could not be seen with it without occasioning public remark, she was forced, though much against her will, to heed his wishes, and enjoy its brilliancy in private. But once, when he was out of town, she dared to appear with this fortune on her breast, and again while on a visit West,—and her husband heard of it.

Mr. Fairbrother had had the jewel set to suit him, not in Florence, as Sears had said, but by a skilful workman he had picked up in great poverty in a remote corner of Williamsburg. Always in dread of some complication, he had provided himself with a second facsimile in paste, this time of an astonishing brightness, and this facsimile he had had set precisely like the true stone. Then he gave the workman a thousand dollars and sent him back to Switzerland. This imitation in paste he showed nobody, but he kept it always in his pocket; why, he hardly knew. Meantime, he had one confidant, not of his crime, but of his sentiments toward his wife, and the determination he had secretly made to proceed to extremities if she continued to disobey him.

This was a man of his own age or older, who had known him in his early days, and had followed all his fortunes. He had been the master of Fairbrother then, but he was his servant now, and as devoted to his interests as if they were his own,—which, in a way, they were. For eighteen years he had stood at the latter's right hand, satisfied to look no further, but, for the last three, his glances had strayed a foot or two beyond his master, and taken in his master's wife.

The feelings which this man had for Mrs. Fairbrother were peculiar. She was a mere adjunct to her great lord, but she was a very gorgeous one, and, while he could not imagine himself doing anything to thwart him whose bread he ate, and to whose rise he had himself contributed, yet if he could remain true to him without injuring her, he would account himself happy. The day came when he had to decide between them, and, against all chances, against his own preconceived notion of what he would do under these circumstances, he chose to consider her.

This day came when, in the midst of growing complacency and an intense interest in some new scheme which demanded all his powers, Abner Fairbrother learned from the papers that Mr. Grey, of English Parliamentary fame, had arrived in New York on an indefinite visit. As no cause was assigned for the visit beyond a natural desire on the part of this eminent statesman to see this great country, Mr. Fairbrother's fears reached a sudden climax, and he saw himself ruined and for ever disgraced if the diamond now so unhappily out of his hands should fall under the eyes of its owner, whose seeming quiet under its loss had not for a moment deceived him. Waiting only long enough to make sure that the distinguished foreigner was likely to accept social attentions, and so in all probability would be brought in contact with Mrs. Fairbrother, he sent her by his devoted servant a peremptory message, in which he demanded back his diamond; and, upon her refusing to heed this, followed it up by another, in which he expressly stated that if she took it out of the safe deposit in which he had been told she was wise enough to keep it, or wore it so much as once during the next three months, she would pay for her presumption with her life.

This was no idle threat, though she chose to regard it as such, laughing in the old servant's face and declaring that she would run the risk if the notion seized her. But the notion did not seem to seize her at once, and her husband was beginning to take heart, when he heard of the great ball about to be given by the Ramsdells and realized that if she were going to be tempted to wear the diamond at all, it would be at this brilliant function given in honor of the one man he had most cause to fear in the whole world.

Sears, seeing the emotion he was under, watched him closely. They had both been on the point of starting for New Mexico to visit a mine in which Mr. Fairbrother was interested, and he waited with inconceivable anxiety to see if his master would change his plans. It was while he was in this condition of mind that he was seen to shake his fist at Mrs. Fairbrother's passing figure; a menace naturally interpreted as directed against her, but which, if we know the man, was rather the expression of his anger against the husband who could rebuke and threaten so beautiful a creature. Meanwhile, Mr. Fairbrother's preparations went on and, three weeks before the ball, they started. Mr. Fairbrother had business in Chicago and business in Denver. It was two weeks and more before he reached La Junta. Sears counted the days. At La Junta they had a long conversation; or rather Mr. Fairbrother talked and Sears listened. The sum of what he said was this: He had made up his mind to have back his diamond. He was going to New York to get it. He was going alone, and as he wished no one to know that he had gone or that his plans had been in any way interrupted, the other was to continue on to El Moro, and, passing himself off as Fairbrother, hire a room at the hotel and shut himself up in it for ten days on any plea his ingenuity might suggest. If at the end of that time Fairbrother should rejoin him, well and good. They would go on together to Santa Fe. But if for any reason the former should delay his return, then Sears was to exercise his own judgment as to the length of time he should retain his borrowed personality; also as to the advisability of pushing on to the mine and entering on the work there, as had been planned between them.

Sears knew what all this meant. He understood what was in his master's mind, as well as if he had been taken into his full confidence, and openly accepted his part of the business with seeming alacrity, even to the point of supplying Fairbrother with suitable references as to the ability of one James

Wellgood to fill a waiter's place at fashionable functions. It was not the first he had given him. Seventeen years before he had written the same, minus the last phrase. That was when he was the master and Fairbrother the man. But he did not mean to play the part laid out for him, for all his apparent acquiescence. He began by following the other's instructions. He exchanged clothes with him and other necessaries, and took the train for La Junta at or near the time that Fairbrother started east. But once at El Moro—once registered there as Abner Fairbrother from New York—he took a different course from the one laid out for him,—a course which finally brought him into his master's wake and landed him at the same hour in New York.

This is what he did. Instead of shutting himself up in his room he expressed an immediate desire to visit some neighboring mines, and, procuring a good horse, started off at the first available moment. He rode north, lost himself in the mountains, and wandered till he found a guide intelligent enough to lend himself to his plans. To this guide he confided his horse for the few days he intended to be gone, paying him well and promising him additional money if, during his absence, he succeeded in circulating the report that he, Abner Fairbrother, had gone deep into the mountains, bound for such and such a camp.

Having thus provided an alibi, not only for himself, but for his master, too, in case he should need it, he took the direct road to the nearest railway station, and started on his long ride east. He did not expect to overtake the man he had been personating, but fortune was kinder than is usual in such cases, and, owing to a delay caused by some accident to a freight train, he arrived in Chicago within a couple of hours of Mr. Fairbrother, and started out of that city on the same train. But not on the same car. Sears had caught a glimpse of Fairbrother on the platform, and was careful to keep out of his sight. This was easy enough. He bought a compartment in the sleeper and stayed in it till they arrived at the Grand Central Station. Then he hastened out and, fortune favoring him with another glimpse of the man in whose movements he was so interested, followed him into the streets.

Fairbrother had shaved off his beard before leaving El Moro. Sears had shaved his off on the train. Both were changed, the former the more, owing to a peculiarity of his mouth which up till now he had always thought best to cover. Sears, therefore, walked behind him without fear, and was almost at his heels when this owner of one of New York's most notable mansions, entered, with a spruce air, the doors of a prominent caterer.

Understanding the plot now, and having everything to fear for his mistress, he walked the streets for some hours in a state of great indecision. Then he went up to her apartment. But he had no sooner come within sight of it than a sense of disloyalty struck him and he slunk away, only to come sidling back when it was too late and she had started for the ball.

Trembling with apprehension, but still strangely divided in his impulses, wishing to serve master and mistress both, without disloyalty to the one or injury to the other, he hesitated and argued with himself, till his fears for the latter drove him to Mr. Ramsdell's house.

The night was a stormy one. The heaviest snow of the season was falling with a high gale blowing down the Sound. As he approached the house, which, as we know, is one of the modern ones in the Riverside district, he felt his heart fail him. But as he came nearer and got the full effect of glancing lights, seductive music, and the cheery bustle of crowding carriages, he saw in his mind's eye such a picture of his beautiful mistress, threatened, unknown to herself, in a quarter she little realized, that he lost all sense of what had hitherto deterred him. Making then and there his great choice, he looked about for the entrance, with the full intention of seeing and warning her.

But this, he presently perceived, was totally impracticable. He could neither go to her nor expect her to come to him; meanwhile, time was passing, and if his master was there—The thought made his head dizzy, and, situated as he was, among the carriages, he might have been run over in his confusion if his eyes had not suddenly fallen on a lighted window, the shade of which had been inadvertently left up.

Within this window, which was only a few feet above his head, stood the glowing image of a woman clad in pink and sparkling with jewels. Her face was turned from him, but he recognized her splendor as that of the one woman who could never be too gorgeous for his taste; and, alive to this unexpected opportunity, he made for this window with the intention of shouting up to her and so attracting her attention.

But this proved futile, and, driven at last to the end of his resources, he tore out a slip of paper from his note-book and, in the dark and with the blinding snow in his eyes, wrote the few broken sentences which he thought would best warn her, without compromising his master. The means he took to reach her with this note I have already related. As soon as he saw it in her hands he fled the place and took the first train west. He was in a pitiable condition, when, three days later, he reached the small station from which he had originally set out. The haste, the exposure, the horror of the crime he had failed to avert, had undermined his hitherto excellent constitution, and the symptoms of a serious illness were beginning to make themselves manifest. But he, like his indomitable master, possessed a great fund of energy and willpower. He saw that if he was to save Abner Fairbrother (and now that Mrs. Fairbrother was dead, his old master was all the world to him) he must make Fairbrother's alibi good by carrying on the deception as planned by the latter, and getting as soon as possible to his camp in the New Mexico mountains. He knew that he would have strength to do this and he went about it without sparing himself.

Making his way into the mountains, he found the guide and his horse at the place agreed upon and, paying the guide enough for his services to insure a quiet tongue, rode back toward El Moro where he was met and sent on to Santa Fe as already related.

Such is the real explanation of the well-nigh unintelligible scrawl found in Mrs. Fairbrother's hand after her death. As to the one which left Miss Grey's bedside for this same house, it was, alike in the writing and sending, the loving freak of a very sick but tender-hearted girl. She had noted the look with which Mr. Grey had left her, and, in her delirious state, thought that a line in her own hand would convince him of her good condition and make it possible for him to enjoy the evening. She was, however, too much afraid of her nurse to write it openly, and though we never found that scrawl, it was doubtless not very different in appearance from the one with which I had confounded it. The man to whom it was intrusted stopped for too many warming drinks on his way for it ever to reach Mr. Ramsdell's house. He did not even return home that night, and when he did put in an appearance the next morning, he was dismissed.

This takes me back to the ball and Mrs. Fairbrother. She had never had much fear of her husband till she received his old servant's note in the peculiar manner already mentioned. This, coming through the night and the wet and with all the marks of hurry upon it, did impress her greatly and led her to take the first means which offered of ridding herself of her dangerous ornament. The story of this we know.

Meanwhile, a burning heart and a scheming brain were keeping up their deadly work a few paces off under the impassive aspect and active movements of the caterer's newly-hired waiter. Abner Fairbrother, whose real character no one had ever been able to sound, unless it was the man who had known him in his days of struggle, was one of those dangerous men who can conceal under a still brow and a noiseless manner the most violent passions and the most desperate resolves. He was angry with his wife, who was deliberately jeopardizing his good name, and he had come there to kill her if he found her flaunting the diamond in Mr. Grey's eyes; and though no one could have detected any change in his look and manner as he passed through the room where these two were standing, the doom of that fair woman was struck when he saw the eager scrutiny and indescribable air of recognition with which this long-defrauded gentleman eyed his own diamond.

He had meant to attack her openly, seize the diamond, fling it at Mr. Grey's feet, and then kill himself. That had been his plan. But when he found, after a round or two among the guests, that nobody looked at him, and nobody recognized the well-known millionaire in the automaton-like figure with the formally-arranged whiskers and sleekly-combed hair, colder purposes intervened, and he asked himself if it would not be possible to come upon her alone, strike his blow, possess himself of the diamond, and make for parts unknown before his identity could be discovered. He loved life even without the charm cast over it by this woman. Its struggles and its hard-bought luxuries fascinated him. If Mr. Grey suspected him, why, Mr. Grey was English, and he a resourceful American. If it came to an issue, the subtle American would win if Mr. Grey were not able to point to the flaw which marked this diamond as his own. And this, Fairbrother had provided against, and would succeed in if he could hold his passions in check and be ready with all his wit when matters reached a climax.

Such were the thoughts and such the plans of the quiet, attentive man who, with his tray laden with coffee and ices, came and went an unnoticed unit among twenty other units similarly quiet and similarly attentive. He waited on lady after lady, and when, on the reissuing of Mr. Durand from the alcove, he passed in there with his tray and his two cups of coffee, nobody heeded and nobody remembered.

It was all over in a minute, and he came out, still unnoted, and went to the supper-room for more cups of coffee. But that minute had set its seal on his heart for ever. She was sitting there alone with her side to the entrance, so that he had to pass around in order to face her. Her elegance and a certain air she had of remoteness from the scene of which she was the glowing center when she smiled, awed him and made his hand loosen a little on the slender stiletto he held close against the bottom of the tray. But such resolution does not easily yield, and his fingers soon tightened again, this time with a deadly grip.

He had expected to meet the flash of the diamond as he bent over her, and dreaded doing so for fear it would attract his eye from her face and so cost him the sight of that startled recognition which would give the desired point to his revenge. But the tray, as he held it, shielded her breast from view, and when he lowered it to strike his blow, he thought of nothing but aiming so truly as to need no second blow. He had had his experience in those old years in a mining camp, and he did not fear failure in this. What he did fear was her utterance of some cry,—possibly his name. But she was stunned with horror, and did not shriek,—horror of him whose eyes she met with her glassy and staring ones as he slowly drew forth the weapon.

Why he drew it forth instead of leaving it in her breast he could not say. Possibly because it gave him his moment of gloating revenge. When in another instant, her hands flew up, and the tray tipped, and the china fell, the revulsion came, and his eyes opened to two facts: the instrument of death was still in his grasp, and the diamond, on whose possession he counted, was gone from his wife's breast.

It was a horrible moment. Voices could be heard approaching the alcove,— laughing voices that in an instant would take on the note of horror. And the music,—ah! how low it had sunk, as if to give place to the dying murmur he now heard issuing from her lips. But he was a man of iron. Thrusting the stiletto into the first place that offered, he drew the curtains over the staring windows, then slid out with his tray, calm, speckless and attentive as ever, dead to thought, dead to feeling, but aware, quite aware in the secret depths of his being that something besides his wife had been killed that night, and that sleep and peace of mind and all pleasure in the past were gone for ever.

It was not he I saw enter the alcove and come out with news of the crime. He left this role to one whose antecedents could better bear investigation. His part was to play, with just the proper display of horror and curiosity, the ordinary menial brought face to face with a crime in high life. He could do this. He could even sustain his share in the gossip, and for this purpose kept near the other waiters. The absence of the diamond was all that troubled him. That brought him at times to the point of vertigo. Had Mr. Grey recognized and claimed it? If so, he, Abner Fairbrother, must remain James Wellgood, the waiter, indefinitely. This would require more belief in his star than ever he had had yet. But as the moments passed, and no contradiction was given to the universally-received impression that the same hand which had struck the blow had taken the diamond, even this cause of anxiety left his breast and he faced people with more and more courage till the moment when he suddenly heard that the diamond had been found in the possession of a man perfectly strange to him, and saw the inspector pass it over into the hands of Mr. Grey.

Instantly he realized that the crisis of his fate was on him. If Mr. Grey were given time to identify this stone, he, Abner Fairbrother, was lost and the diamond as well. Could he prevent this? There was but one way, and that way he took. Making use of his ventriloquial powers—he had spent a year on the public stage in those early days, playing just such tricks as these—he raised the one cry which he knew would startle Mr. Grey more than any other in the world, and when the diamond fell from his hand, as he knew it would, he rushed forward and, in the act of picking it up, made that exchange which not only baffled the suspicions of the statesman, but restored to him the diamond, for whose possession he was now ready to barter half his remaining days.

Meanwhile Mr. Grey had had his own anxieties. During this whole long evening, he had been sustained by the conviction that the diamond of which he had caught but one passing glimpse was the Great Mogul of his once famous collection. So sure was he of this, that at one moment he found himself tempted to enter the alcove, demand a closer sight of the diamond and settle the question then and there. He even went so far as to take in his hands the two cups of coffee which should serve as his excuse for this intrusion, but his naturally chivalrous instincts again intervened, and he set the cups down again—this I did not see—and turned his steps toward the library with the intention of writing her a note instead. But though he found paper and pen to hand, he could find no words for so daring a request, and he came back into the hall, only to hear that the woman he had contemplated addressing had just been murdered and her great jewel stolen.

The shock was too much, and as there was no leaving the house then, he retreated again to the library where he devoured his anxieties in silence till hope revived again at sight of the diamond in the inspector's hand, only to vanish under the machinations of one he did not even recognize when he took the false jewel from his hand.

The American had outwitted the Englishman and the triumph of evil was complete.

Or so it seemed. But if the Englishman is slow, he is sure. Thrown off the track for the time being, Mr. Grey had only to see a picture of the stiletto in the papers, to feel again that, despite all appearances, Fairbrother was really not only at the bottom of the thefts from which his cousin and himself had suffered, but of this frightful murder as well. He made no open move—he was a stranger in a strange land and much disturbed, besides, by his fears for his daughter—but he started a secret inquiry through his old valet, whom he ran across in the street, and whose peculiar adaptability for this kind of work he well knew.

The aim of these inquiries was to determine if the person, whom two physicians and three assistants were endeavoring to nurse back to health on the top of a wild plateau in a remote district of New Mexico, was the man he had once entertained at his own board in England, and the adventures thus incurred would make a story in itself. But the result seemed to justify them. Word came after innumerable delays, very trying to Mr. Grey, that he was not the same, though he bore the name of Fairbrother, and was considered by every one around there to be Fairbrother. Mr. Grey, ignorant of the relations between the millionaire master and his man which sometimes led to the latter's personifying the former, was confident of his own mistake and bitterly ashamed of his own suspicions.

But a second message set him right. A deception was being practised down in New Mexico, and this was how his spy had found it out. Certain letters which went into the sick tent were sent away again, and always to one address. He had learned the address. It was that of James Wellgood, C—, Maine. If Mr. Grey would look up this Wellgood he would doubtless learn something of the man he was so interested in.

This gave Mr. Grey personally something to do, for he would trust no second party with a message involving the honor of a possibly innocent man. As the place was accessible by railroad and his duty clear, he took the journey involved and succeeded in getting a glimpse in the manner we know of the man James Wellgood. This time he recognized Fairbrother and, satisfied from the circumstances of the moment that he would be making no mistake in accusing him of having taken the Great Mogul, he intercepted him in his flight, as you have already read, and demanded the immediate return of his great diamond.

And Fairbrother? We shall have to go back a little to bring his history up to this critical instant.

When he realized the trend of public opinion; when he saw a perfectly innocent man committed to the Tombs for his crime, he was first astonished and then amused at what he continued to regard as the triumph of his star. But he did not start for El Moro, wise as he felt it would be to do so. Something of the fascination usual with criminals kept him near the scene of his crime,—that, and an anxiety to see how Sears would conduct himself in the Southwest. That Sears had followed him to New York, knew his crime, and was the strongest witness against him, was as far from his thoughts as that he owed him the warning which had all but balked him of his revenge. When therefore he read in the papers that "Abner Fairbrother" had been found sick in his camp at Santa Fe, he felt that nothing now stood in the way of his entering on the plans he had framed for ultimate escape. On his departure from El Moro he had taken the precaution of giving Sears the name of a certain small town on the coast of Maine where his mail was to be sent in case of a great emergency. He had chosen this town for two reasons. First, because he knew all about it, having had a young man from there in his employ; secondly, because of its neighborhood to the inlet where an old launch of his had been docked for the winter. Always astute, always precautionary, he had given orders to have this launch floated and provisioned, so that now he had only to send word to the captain, to have at his command the best possible means of escape.

Meanwhile, he must make good his position in C—. He did it in the way we know. Satisfied that the only danger he need fear was the discovery of the fraud practised in New Mexico, he had confidence enough in Sears, even in his present disabled state, to take his time and make himself solid with the people of C—while waiting for the ice to disappear from the harbor. This accomplished and cruising made possible, he took a flying trip to New York to secure such papers and valuables as he wished to carry out of the country with him. They were in safe deposit, but that safe deposit was in his strong room in the center of his house in Eighty-sixth Street (a room which you will remember in connection with Sweetwater's adventure). To enter his own door with his own latch-key, in the security and darkness of a stormy night, seemed to this self-confident man a matter of no great risk. Nor did he find it so. He reached his strong room, procured his securities and was leaving the house, without having suffered an alarm, when some instinct of self-preservation suggested to him the advisability of arming himself with a pistol. His own was in Maine, but he remembered where Sears kept his; he had seen it often enough in that old trunk he had brought with him from the Sierras. He accordingly went up stairs to the steward's room, found the pistol and became from that instant invincible. But in restoring the articles he had pulled out he came across a photograph of his wife and lost himself over it and went mad, as we have heard the detective tell. That later, he should succeed in trapping this detective and should leave the house without a qualm as to his fate shows what sort of man he was in moments of extreme danger. I doubt, from what I have heard of him since, if he ever gave two thoughts to the man after he had sprung the double lock on him; which, considering his extreme ignorance of who his victim was or what relation he bore to his own fate, was certainly remarkable.

Back again in C—, he made his final preparations for departure. He had already communicated with the captain of the launch, who may or may not have known his passenger's real name. He says that he supposed him to be some agent of Mr. Fairbrother's; that among the first orders he received from that gentleman was one to the effect that he was to follow the instructions of one Wellgood as if they came from himself; that he had done so, and not till he had Mr. Fairbrother on board had he known whom he was expected to carry into other waters. However, there are many who do not believe the captain. Fairbrother had a genius for rousing devotion in the men who worked for him, and probably this man was another Sears.

To leave speculation, all was in train, then, and freedom but a quarter of a mile away, when the boat he was in was stopped by another and he heard Mr. Grey's voice demanding the jewel.

The shock was severe and he had need of all the nerve which had hitherto made his career so prosperous, to sustain the encounter with the calmness which alone could carry off the situation. Declaring that the diamond was in New York, he promised to restore it if the other would make the sacrifice worth while by continuing to preserve his hitherto admirable silence concerning him: Mr. Grey responded by granting him just twenty-four hours; and when Fairbrother said the time was not long enough and allowed his hand to steal ominously to his breast, he repeated still more decisively, "Twenty-four hours."

The ex-miner honored bravery. Withdrawing his hand from his breast, he brought out a note-book instead of a pistol and, in a tone fully as determined, replied: "The diamond is in a place inaccessible to any one but myself. If you will put your name to a promise not to betray me for the thirty-six hours I ask, I will sign one to restore you the diamond before one-thirty o'clock on Friday."

"I will," said Mr. Grey.

So the promises were written and duly exchanged. Mr. Grey returned to New York and Fairbrother boarded his launch.

The diamond really was in New York, and to him it seemed more politic to use it as a means of securing Mr. Grey's permanent silence than to fly the country, leaving a man behind him who knew his secret and could precipitate his doom with a word. He would, therefore, go to New York, play his last great card and, if he lost, be no worse off than he was now. He did not mean to lose.

But he had not calculated on any inherent weakness in himself,—had not calculated on Providence. A dish tumbled and with it fell into chaos the fair structure of his dreams. With the cry of "Grizel! Grizel!" he gave up his secret, his hopes and his life. There was no retrieval possible after that. The star of Abner Fairbrother had set.

Mr. Grey and his daughter learned very soon of my relations to Mr. Durand, but through the precautions of the inspector and my own powers of self-control, no suspicion has ever crossed their minds of the part I once played in the matter of the stiletto.

This was amply proved by the invitation Mr. Durand and I have just received to spend our honeymoon at Darlington Manor.

Echo Library
www.echo-library.com

Echo Library uses advanced digital print-on-demand technology to build and preserve an exciting world class collection of rare and out-of-print books, making them readily available for everyone to enjoy.

Situated just yards from Teddington Lock on the River Thames, Echo Library was founded in 2005 by Tom Cherrington, a specialist dealer in rare and antiquarian books with a passion for literature.

Please visit our website for a complete catalogue of our books, which includes foreign language titles.

The Right to Read

Echo Library actively supports the Royal National Institute of the Blind's Right to Read initiative by publishing a comprehensive range of large print and clear print titles.

Large Print titles are in 16 point Tiresias font as recommended by the RNIB.

Clear Print titles are in 13 point Tiresias font and designed for those who find standard print difficult to read.

Customer Service

If there is a serious error in the text or layout please send details to feedback@echo-library.com and we will supply a corrected copy. If there is a printing fault or the book is damaged please refer to your supplier.

Lightning Source UK Ltd.
Milton Keynes UK
16 February 2011

167569UK00001B/125/P